WATCHER
UNFEIGNED

Dark Angels Paranormal Romance

JL MADORE

JL Madore

www.jlmadore.com

Cover Design: Fiona Jayde Media

Copy Edit: Jenn Wood, All About the Edits

Book Layout © 2017 BookDesignTemplates.com

Note: The moral right of the author has been asserted.

Watcher Unfeigned/ JL Madore -- 1st ed.

ISBN 978-1-989187-48-7

Author Note:

Welcome to book seven of the Watchers of the Gray, Dark Angels Paranormal Series – Watcher Unfeigned.

This series is written to be read in order. I follow up with each of the couples as a family saga as we move through their lives and you'll enjoy the story more if you have context. If you haven't started at the beginning, Zander is your man in book 1 – Watcher Untethered

If you're all set to jump into the following pages, then enjoy. Devour the struggles and triumphs of Zander and his warrior brothers. When you've finished, continue the journey with the next books:

The Watchers of the Gray Series (Paranormal)
Book 1 – Watcher Untethered (Zander)
Book 2 – Watcher Redeemed (Kyrian)
Book 3 – Watcher Reborn (Danel)
Book 4 – Watcher Divided (Phoenix)
Book 5 – Watcher United (Seth)
Book 6 – Watcher Compelled (Bo)
Book 7 – Watcher Unfeigned (Brennus)
Book 8 – Watcher Exposed (Hark)

CHAPTER ONE

a fine line separated a deeply concerned friend-with-benefits from an obsessed stalker. Brennus feared he pole-vaulted over that line with Colton Creed weeks ago. Was he dead? Had feeding from him killed the cop? Was he suffering somewhere, alone and in trouble? Had his Seraph side poisoned him?

"Stay the fuck away from me, Celt." The cerulean blue of Colt's glowing eyes haunted him in both his waking hours and his sleep. He felt the piercing bite of his extended fangs in his throat, the desperate pull on his vein as the guy groaned against his neck.

How could they have gone from savage good sex to the cop falling off the face of the earth one moment later?

No forwarding address. No calls returned.

He took an indefinite leave at the police station.

His cousin had no idea where he was—or wasn't telling.

Members of the Darkworld knew better than to feed off Nephilim. Brennus was born of a human woman and an Archangel asshole. What ran in his veins was caustic to daemons nine times outta ten. It was acid—poison.

1

But there had been no stopping him.

After Colt delivered on his promise of a mind-numbing blowjob, he lunged at him more demon than man. Brennus assplanted in that alley with the cop on top of him and the male's canines punctured his flesh.

He protested, pushing at the male's chest, but who was he kidding—the two of them got off on the danger of the forbidden. They were nitroglycerine and an earthquake.

Colt didn't heed the danger, grinding on him, feeding in gluttonous pulls. The male was nothing but sex.

Nothing but need.

And Sweet Lady forgive him, Brennus lost his mind as well. He should've fought harder and thrown the male against the next building for his own good. Instead, he got the male's pants open and stroked him off.

He thought they were all right when the cop shuddered, coming in violent waves. Not once, not twice, but in multiple convulsions of a sticky cum that chilled Brennus's skin and smelled like a heady musk.

The unique scent woke something sexy inside him.

Then shit went sideways. Colt leapt to his feet, covered in blood and cum and filth from rolling on the ground in that alley. He looked feral. *"Stay the fuck away from me, Celt."*

Brennus tipped back his flask and took a solid swig. He really needed to slow down on the liquid sedation, but he was right close to being out of his head with worry.

He hadn't seen the male since that night. Not for lack of trying. The Ice Demon was just gone. Vapor.

What if his blood *did* poison him? What if the daemon overtook the male and he was still feral somewhere? He honestly didn't know what went wrong or how to make it right.

"Celt?" Seth's voice came through his earpiece. "You still with us, my brother?"

Brennus got his head back into the game and finished the

energy sweep of the abandoned warehouse. The metal and glass structure was cavernous, but they only used an area at the back, so the job was simple.

When life, human or Otherworld, came to a truly violent and horrible end, it left a negative imprint of energy. That tended to draw more ill-meaning Dark-worlders and malicious intent—a siren's call of the residual power. That bad juju needed clearing up before they walked away, or they'd end up with another slaughter on their hands.

"All clear, Egyptian. We're good to shut this one down."

Brennus shut off his Otherworld gift and retreated to where the twins waited for him out by the road. After a mass killing of Darkworlders a few weeks ago, they assembled the bodies of the victims in this warehouse to allow families of missing daemons to identify the salvaged remains.

Unfortunately, without heads, nailing down the identities of the victims became more of a guessing game than a science. If they didn't get these bad guys soon, they'd need a forensic scientist on the team.

"All the evil mojo clear?" Seth sipped at the rim of a Tim's cup as he joined them.

The Egyptian twins created an impressive sight. Physically identical, the two massive warriors, with their skull-trimmed hair, ebony wings, and their red leather trenches and boots were something to behold.

Massive and muscled, these mountains of their garrison gave any troublemakers pause.

"Aye," Brennus said, falling into step as they made their way back to the busier city streets to patrol. "We were lucky Gheil put us in touch with a Necromancer Shade that could consume the tainted energy."

Seth shook out his empty cup and stuffed it into the long pocket at his hip until they found a street side garbage can. "We wouldn't have to go through the Djinn Master for a cleanup if the cop wasn't AWOL. Where the fuck is Colt?"

Brennus shrugged, nausea churning in his gut. "I wish I knew. I honestly wish I knew."

Phoenix lifted his hands and started signing. *Hey, if you guys have things nailed down, I'd like to head over to the hotel and escort Storme home.*

Brennus's mood lifted at the mention of visiting Storme at work. Phoenix's wife was finishing off the details for the grand opening of the newest location of the boutique, Queen Hotel. After inheriting the business from her batshit mentor and then marrying Phoenix, she relocated the head office to the heart of Toronto. The lass was pulling long hours to ensure success . . . and so was her lovely assistant, Jack.

"Aye, that's a fine idea, Phoenix. Let us tag along to see the progress." Brennus changed their direction, not about to take no for an answer. "Then yer brother and I will get back to keepin' the streets safe for the innocents of mankind, and you can see your fair lady safe home."

Seth raised a dark brow, but for once in his life, kept his mouth clamped shut.

Well, would wonders never cease?

Seth found his off button.

$\sim$

Zander walked shoulder to shoulder with Danel through the late-night sports enthusiasts, club goers, and end of the night train catchers. May was a decent month for weather in TO. The changing seasons freed humans from their environmentally imposed hibernation. Spring rains washed away the bitter cold of winter. The intermittent days of sun warmed up the evenings that followed. The world sprang to life once more.

As much as he appreciated the return to more hospitable

conditions, the rise in temperature made the nightly grind harder. More bodies on the streets meant more potential Darkworld infractions to police and thus, a higher risk of exposure.

They turned west, the heavy, rubber soles of their boots eating up the pavement as they wandered a stretch of deserted buildings along the lakefront. The streets had been quiet of Darkworld activity since the totem pole slaughter and the raid on their home two weeks ago.

Whether the Red-Metal Rebellion had taken a crippling blow due to the men lost, or the scum of Hell had coiled up in a corner somewhere lamenting their losses and plotting their next strike, they had no clue.

Didn't matter. Either way, they'd continue to do what they always did—night after night after night.

"Thanks for taking Sunshine out this afternoon," D said.

Zander thought about his afternoon, and the warmth of his growing family bloomed in his chest. The sun had been out, the birds singing, and he'd looked at that little blonde angel staring out the window at the horses, and it had melted his heart. "We share a love of horses, she and I. It was my pleasure to saddle up and take her for a ride. She's a sweet kid."

Danel nodded. The lack of biological connection didn't mean a thing to the warrior. He and his beast had taken one look at Sunshine and plummeted head first in love with the little waif. "Can you believe where we are, Z? Some nights, I'm afraid to breathe. Like, if I disturb the scene, it'll all go up on me, and I'll be left with nothing but fate's mocking laughter."

Zander knew that sensation all too well.

He was a year longer into the wedded bliss and family life than Danel, Ronnie, and now little Sunshine, and it still caught him off guard most nights. "More to love is more to lose. All we can do is take it one night at a time and protect what Lady Divinity blessed us with."

Zander sent up a wave of devotion to their patron mother, and by Danel's glance to the night sky, he did the same.

Who'd have believed this, right? Danel and he not only able to share a shift but chat about life and love. Shit, they'd come a *loooong* way from the dark place they'd each been.

He'd never bring it up and hadn't realized he cared, but endless centuries of Danel despising him had weighed heavy on his heart and soul. Thanks to the love of females, they were whole and healed.

"I've got lawyers working on securing Sunshine's place with us," he said, checking the sightlines and the vacant windows looking out at them. "Humans have laws and waiting periods and home visits and things to maneuver, but my guys don't foresee a problem."

"Thanks, Z. Seriously. I have no patience with the idea of being judged by humans over this or the threat that they might think they can take her away from us. My beast would rip them to shreds."

Zander got that. If anyone threatened to take Niobi from him and Austin, he'd raze the earth to cinders. "We won't tip anyone off. As far as we've found out, she isn't in any system and has no kin to come looking for her."

Danel swallowed, his head bobbing. "Good. That's good to hear."

"Everything's gonna work out, Persian. You'll see." Zander's phone buzzed against his hip. As he took in Tanek's text, his heart didn't so much stop as freeze in his chest.

911-Ronnie. Get D home now.

Fucking fate. It just *had* to shit on them.

~

Colt was in Hell—literally. Burning fires scorched his flesh and blackened his lungs with layers of rancid sulphur. His wrists were shackled, stretching him out like a full-monty starfish over a bed of hot syringe needles, his shifting weight injecting him with an evil medley of toxins. His skin was on fire, fighting against the sub-zero burn of the icy powers pulsing in his cells.

Utterly excruciating—and he ate up the agony.

How long had he been there? A week? A year? Time was a fickle fuck in Hell. The torturous days and hours stretched on and yet never got anywhere. Didn't matter. He deserved every ounce of pain. Welcomed it.

Fucking around with a Nephilim was beyond stupid. It threatened everything he was—everything he wanted to be. But to feed on him? To take the Celt's blood into his body?

He'd lost his cock-driven mind.

"Have you had enough, sire? Can we leave this place and be done with this?"

Colt shook his head but got nowhere because his skull was locked in place and strapped down. "I need more. I can't . . . you have to make it stop. I won't leave until I am myself again."

His assigned Hell servant shrugged. "As you wish."

〜

Brennus led their trio as he and the twins headed over toward Storme's new hotel. His focus had shifted from the quiet still-ness of the streets to prep his charming Hi-how-are-ya for young Jack. He promised the lad a private tour of the town a few weeks ago, and he was in the mood to make good on his plans. Or, they could skip the meal and start with a tour of one of the new hotel rooms.

You know, to test out the mattress for quality assurance.

The scent of blood on the wind had his head cranking around and he signaled for the twins to halt. The copper in the air wasn't a skinned knee kinda scent. The strength of the perfume promised a perforated, leaking body and plasma pooling into puddles.

Seth flipped into fight mode a nanosecond later and drew his gun. The Egyptian mountains of muscle pushed past to take the lead, and Brennus fell in behind him.

Down a cramped and littered service lane, they wove their way behind a series of low-rise office buildings. The grunts and thuds of distant fighting bounced down the concrete funnel of the alley, and things got more intense: the darkness of the shadows, the tang of spilled blood, the need to know what they were walking into.

He tapped the video-link on the front of his vest. "I've got you, boys," Tanek said over their comm system. "Thanks for the invite to the party."

Pop. Pop.

Gunshots went off up ahead, and the three of them beat feet and broke into a run. They didn't have a visual yet, but the shots echoed from less than a full city block away. Left. Straight. They took a right into another alley-artery and ended up bursting in on a whole lotta messed up. Shiiiite.

Back-flatting against a red brick wall, they dropped into defensive shooting positions. Phoenix tucked in behind a green industrial dumpster, Seth stepped into the back door stoop of one of the buildings, and he rolled and crouched behind a stack of skids.

Brennus missed the days of invincibility, when they burst into every scenario as indestructible motherfuckers and took out the trash. Now, one red-metal bullet to the head could take them off the playing field for good.

Engagement protocols changed.

Caution became part of their nights.

Oh, how he missed the good ole days.

Brennus popped his head above the skids and took a quick

gopher gawk at what they were dealing with before ducking back down. It was a clusterfuck—a Downworlder Donnybrook.

And for once, they weren't the targets.

"So, what say you, boys?" he asked, meeting the gaze of the twins. "Shall we break it up or simply observe and let the chips fall?"

"Door number two," Seth said. "It's contained. No sightline. And really, none of our business. Let's wait and—"

A stray bullet—either from a ricochet down the alley or from one of the three new daemons running past to join the party—caught Brennus in the shoulder. The kick knocked him back, and the blaze of pain brought him into clear focus.

His beast lit up.

"Fucking hell," he cursed, twisting to check the back of his jacket for an exit. "Straight through. I'm good."

Not as good as he would've been if he'd made it to the hotel and met up with Jack. Yep. The universe always nailed you in the nuts when you let your guard down.

Best-laid plans and all that.

The late arrivals must have tipped off the masses to the Watchers skulking in the shadows because all of a sudden, the welcoming committee came at them from all sides.

"It's amazing how fast the tide turns, isn't it?" Seth said, looking genuinely offended. "And we were minding our own."

Brennus agreed but didn't have time to say so. He returned fire, nailing one attacker in the head as the horde closed in. The force of bullet-through-skull spun the fucker around and he dominoed back, knocking the two behind him staggering.

Leaving the body to fall where it may, he burst forward and took advantage of Newton's Law.

Those objects in motion would stay in motion.

Until they never moved again.

The throbbing burn seeping into his chest told him these

Darkworlders were armed with red-metal. Life or death was new to them, but boy did it ramp up the adrenaline.

Running full-tilt at the off-balance stumblers, he took advantage of their unsteady footing and tackled them both to the ground. The razor-sharp blade of his Crystalline dagger found purchase in the chest of one and then across the throat of the other. Black blood splattered back on him and poured free from the wounds.

He rolled back to his feet and took in the fight.

Seth was busy with hand-to-hand and three opponents, while Phoenix cut through the latest crop of bad guys like a reaper with a scythe. Seriously, the guy had manifested some kind of dark magic scythe and was sweeping that curved blade through the enemy like a murderous farmer in a wheat field.

Except that wasn't wheat falling to the ground.

Someone jumped on Brennus's back and started clawing at his face. He cursed, closing his eyes, his beast really getting pissed. The only males who got to ride him were the ones with his personal invitation.

And when had this devolved into catfighting?

Gunshots and stab wounds were one thing, but targeting a male's face—that was personal.

Reaching over his head, he grabbed the guy by the hair, bent forward, and yanked him over his shoulder. He hissed as the fucker stuck him deep with a blade. The sharp, stabbing pain worsened as he tried to breathe.

Fuck. Punctured lung.

With his fingers still fisted in the asshole's hair, he drew his dagger across the guy's neck and tossed his head across the alley. Clutching his chest, he slipped in a pool of blood and went down hard . . . blade still lodged in his back.

He tried to breathe, ready for the influx of dark energy from his three kills. Normally, he'd fight through the invasion, but with his current status, he would black out.

Lack of oxygen. Red-metaled blade lodged in his back.

More enemies closing in.

When the black mist invaded his eyes and nose, he gasped, staring up at the night sky. A Rugaru bent over him, the hairy motherfucker smiling at his good fortune.

Sloppy seconds, asshole. Ye might get the kill, but ye don't deserve it. Brennus tried to lift his gun, but the thing flopped at his side. Well shit. This wasn't the end he envisioned.

He had things to see, males to do. He wasn't done. Or maybe he was.

CHAPTER TWO

$\mathcal{B}$o arrived on scene just in time to see Brennus go limp. His new Dark Angel side burst forward. Striding hard toward the Rugaru gloating over his fallen brother, he shot a chunk of lead through the back of the asshole's hairy head. He'd never hated a race as a whole before, but after recovering his memories of his recent captive torture session, the Rugaru would be the ones he hated most.

Securing the Celt, he tapped his earpiece and activated his comm. "Brennus is down. We need Kyrian here now."

Tanek responded and got busy calling for their Dark Angel field medic.

Bo dropped to a knee and assessed Brennus's injuries. The warrior was pale as shit and barely breathing. He had an entry hole on his shoulder. He eased him over to—good, the bullet passed right through. So, what . . .

He saw the hilt of the red-metal blade buried between the Celt's ribs. Gripping it hard, he yanked it free and hoped the guy's heavenly healing could take hold.

"Come on, Celt. Stay with us."

Emergency sirens in the distance promised the arrival of human complications.

"We haven't got time to play, boys," he said, drawing his dagger. He laid Brennus down to heal and started with the cleanup. In a hurry, he dragged the bodies of the fallen into a pile, decapitated each of the Darkworlders, and threw their noggins on the pile.

Seth brought a couple more over while Phoenix secured the alley and checked for anything they missed.

Bo lit their haystack of dead, and the ode to charbroiled Darkworlder filled the air. "Shit, we're almost out of time. This ain't gonna burn in time."

The sirens wailed louder now and would weave their way to them any moment.

Phoenix joined them, spread his ebony wings and raised his hands like something you saw in the movies. The pile of dead went up in a roar of crackling blue flames.

"What the hell?" Bo said, backing away from the singeing heat. "You've been hanging out with the dragons too much."

Seth laughed, gathering the weapons and shoving them in his duffle. "Maybe he's got a line on his inner Johnny Storm and decided to Human Torch us outta this mess. Who cares? That bonfire saved us oodles of time."

Kyrian dropped from the sky in a whisper of feathers and Bo jogged back to Brennus and their most pressing problem. "He's bad, Greek. Through-and-through to the shoulder, red-metal blade to the ribs. His breathing is shallow and jerky. I pulled the blade. He should've stabilized by now."

The sirens were right on top of them, and they didn't have a moment to waste. Kyrian scooped up Brennus and shot into the night sky. Bo was new to the Dark Angel transition and hadn't practiced the whole flying yet.

Better to avoid a public scene and dematerialize.

He whistled the all clear and Phoenix flashed a thumbs-up before dissolving into the ether. The scene was a scorched, black tarred, bullet-ridden mess, but there was no risk of Otherworld exposure that he could see.

As long as Brennus pulled through, they'd call it a win.

~

Danel burst through the front door of their ranch home, his heart pounding out of his chest. *911 Ronnie.* What the fuck did that mean? Was his wife hurt? Had she had an accident? A relapse of that fucking disease she suffered from before him?

"Ronnie?" He didn't mean for his voice to boom so loud, but he wasn't firing on all cylinders. His footing faltered when he eyed the **VH** -monogrammed suitcases sitting in the ornate foyer, and a bomb went off in his chest.

His mind raced through their parting only a few hours ago. They hadn't fought. Things were good—weren't they?

"Ronnie?" His vision fritzed as he tracked his beautiful mate and raced to find her. Launching straight up the open air of the stairwell, he hit the second floor and beat feet toward their suite.

Was she leaving him? Why? What had he fucked up?

Ronnie raced down the hall, tears streaming and arms outstretched. She hit his chest without stopping, and he tried to cushion the blow. Thankfully, she'd gained some weight since they'd wed, but she still felt too tiny and fragile in his arms.

She embraced him like the fiercest of bears—which was fabulous. Okay, obviously not leaving him.

Thank you, sweet Lady.

The sorrowful scent of her tears brought his beast roaring to the surface, and he tried not to lose his shit. "What happened? Who do I need to kill to make this better for you?"

She pulled back, her eyes red and puffy. "Daddy had a stroke. They don't think he'll live. I've got to go."

It took a second for that to register. Howton Hennington had a stroke? That man was strong, healthy. How could he be dying? "We'll catch the next flight. I'll find something and—"

She shook her head. "Bentley sent the jet the moment the ambulance left. It'll be there by the time I get there."

"By the time *we* get there," he corrected. "Where you go, I go. If you're facing anything in this life, I'm right beside you."

Her features tightened, and he didn't like the look on her. "But everything is such a mess right now. You're needed here."

He pressed his hand to her heart and bent down to meet her eye to eye. "I'm needed here, first and foremost. You are my priority, baby—my only priority. I won't be separated from you. I swore I'd make love to you every day for the rest of our lives to keep you healthy. I'm a male of my word."

Her smile eased some of his beast's panic, but she didn't look convinced. "I'm sure a few days won't pull me out of remission. Your super-healing spunk is very powerful. I've never felt so strong.

He chuckled that she still called it that.

The fact that he transferred his healing ability to her during sex, and her disease was held at bay, was only part of his need to stay with her. "I love you, Veronica Rose Hennington. I am your husband, your mate, and your protector. My place is at your side. There's no other option. Zander will understand that. Now, you're wasting time. Let's pack me a bag and—"

Movement up the hall had him realizing they had another issue to figure out. "Hey, Sunshine. Are you okay, little one?"

He knelt on the plush carpet and scooped his sleepy little angel into his arms. She was crying too and her tears ruined him as deeply as his wife's. "I made Ronnie sad."

Ronnie gasped, and he got them walking back to his suite.

"No, you did nothing to make her sad. Her daddy is sick. That's not your fault."

Sunshine didn't look convinced. He sat on the end of the sofa in their suite and cuddled his little goldilocks into his lap. "You are the biggest joy in our life, sweet girl. You are our Sunshine when skies are gray."

"Why can't I come? Ronnie says I hasta stay here. I never be'd on a airplane. I want to go."

Ronnie sank to her knees before them, and another round of tears started up. "My daddy's going to go with the angels, baby. I'm going to be sad. You're still sad from your mommy leaving . . . I don't want you to have to go through that again."

"If I'm sad and you sad, why can't we be sad together?"

"We can," Danel said, leaning forward and pulling both his girls in for a family hug. "You help Ronnie pack us a bag, monkey, and I'll go make the arrangements."

"But—" Ronnie started.

Danel shook his head. "I've got you both. I swear. We get through this as a family. No one gets left behind."

~

Storme was losing her mind. Racing out of the parking lot of her new hotel, her skin tingled, responding to the massive flux of her husband's dark magic. Even from blocks away, bound as his witch familiar, she felt the strength of his struggle. Most nights, Phoenix absorbed the crashing waves of his powers like the heroic warrior his transition made him.

It was the nights things got away on him that scared her.

Scared all of them, really.

The transitioned Dark Angel possessed a level of power greater than anything they knew how to contain. Not long ago, Phoenix had levitated an entire warehouse to save Seth, and then took out Kyrian, Zander, and himself with an unexpected pulse of unharnessed energy.

Only two weeks ago, Zander caused a city-wide blackout when he let the buildup of his power loose. The humans were probably *still* trying to figure out what blew their grid. That would be super-Nephilim sex. Oops.

"Are you sure you don't mind the detour?" she asked Jack, glancing over to the passenger seat of her car.

"No. It's fine." He smiled at her, and she wondered how much about the Otherworld he'd gleaned. They never discussed anything Wiccan or other, but he must wonder about things he'd seen over the years. "I'm in no hurry to get back to an empty apartment. The stacked boxes will still be there whenever I get home. Besides, I appreciate getting a ride in your new car."

Her new car. That she was allowed to drive herself home was a major win in her battle for independence. Phoenix and his warrior brothers were wildly protective of their family. After the nosedive off the expressway, there was talk of her being escorted every time she left the ranch.

Yeah, a big hells-no to that one.

The compromise was Phoenix buying her a fully custom, armor-plated, bullet-proof glassed, roll-cage framed, luxury sedan. A tank in Mercedes clothing.

"Phoenix said he wanted to escort me home. That he didn't come and didn't respond to my text has me worried." Not to mention, the surge of dark magic polluting the downtown core.

Jack sat back and watched the city streets pass by.

The nav system signaled an incoming call, and she hit accept before she read who it was.

"Miss Queen, I caught you at last."

Storme rolled her eyes and stuck her tongue out, making Jack giggle in the seat beside her. "Mr. Logan, yes, it's good to finally connect with you. Although, I'm driving and need to keep it short. You understand, distracted driving kills."

17

She slowed at a light and watched an overly amorous couple grope their way across the crosswalk. Phoenix was the topic on her mind. She had no interest in being bullied by a man who didn't want to accept change.

"I was speaking to the other board members and wanted to reach out, once again. Your mother understood—"

"Cleo Queen wasn't my mother." Thank the goddess for that. The woman was actually Phoenix's mother and not at all the female Storme thought her to be. She was selfish and cruel and hurt people she loved.

"Be that as it may, Cleo understood the concept of strength in numbers, and the advantage to having investors backing a business. Which, if I might say, can be a volatile industry at the best of times."

Storme rolled her eyes again. "I thank you for your concern, Mr. Logan. From here out, all future hotels will be privately owned and run. You'll have to survive on the fortune you're already making on the existing locations."

"This isn't about the money, Storme," he said, the fake indignation almost too much to bear.

"Of course it is," she said, interrupting him. "Thanks for your call, Jim. Like I said, the decision is made. See you at the next board meeting."

She tapped "End call," and exhaled. "Blowhard."

"Do you think that'll be the end of him?"

She shook her head. "Not at all. He's a boy's club bully. He'll be hovering a while yet before he gets the picture."

The *bloop* of a text message coming in sounded at the same time Phoenix's name popped up on her nav screen. She hit "Read" and then hoped, too late, that the message was suitable for mixed company.

Sorry, kitten. The Celt is down. Just arrived at the clinic.

Okay. As relieved as she was that Phoenix was good, now she was worried about—

"The Celt?" Jack said, his warm brown eyes locking on her. "Is that Brennus? What does that mean—he's down."

How to explain this? She pulled up to the first gate at the old racetrack and clicked the opener on the visor above her head. After she passed through and the iron rails locked tight behind her, she opened her window and reached out to the keypad. With her security code punched in, she laid her palm over the scanner, and progressed through the second gate.

"You've seen them. You realize they are soldiers, right?"

Jack nodded. "What I can't figure out is, what branch of the military . . . or if they're private . . . or maybe mercenaries."

Good. So, he had considered this.

She rounded the track oval and bypassed the house. "I assure you, they aren't mercenaries. Their primary objective is to safeguard citizens from the evils that go bump in the night. That's really all I can tell you."

Jack nodded. "But they're the good guys?"

Her headlights washed the side of the clinic, and her tires crunched over the white gravel stones. She pulled to a stop and shut the car off. "They are definitely the good guys, but they live through a lot of bad things, so the rest of us don't have to. Does that make sense?"

Storme waited until Jack nodded and then got out, not surprised when he jumped out of the other side. When he rounded the hood, she turned and jogged to the clinic door. Before she got to the handle of what was once the veterinary clinic of the racetrack, the door popped wide, and there he was —her warrior.

Phoenix blocked her vision from everything else around them, and it had nothing to do with his size. It was the same every time they reconnected. It didn't matter if they'd been separated for minutes or hours, when he appeared before her, there was no building, no other brothers, no stars in the night sky—the only thing she saw was him.

Hey kitten, he said, his words a gentle caress in her mind. *I'm glad you're home. And I see you brought a friend.*

She hugged her man around the waist and pressed her cheek against his shirt. Fresh from their closet, it smelled like fabric softener and wasn't the same blue as the shirt he had on when he left tonight.

She never mentioned his little attempts to keep her from facing the remnants of his nights. It was just another way he tried to protect her from the evils of his world.

Pulling back, she probed his magic and assured herself he was whole and that his power held steady.

I'm fine, love. Come inside.

She slid an arm around his waist, and the two of them walked in step, down the wide, tiled corridor. "How is he?"

∾

"I'm fine, lass. I thank ye for askin'." Brennus did the old man shuffle up the hall, feeling every one of his eighteen hundred years of age. Nauseous, shaky as shit, and with his head playing an aggressive game of spinny-top, he ambulated on stubborn pride alone. With one hand braced against the wall and the other swatting away his agitated, fuchsia-haired surgeon, he made the slowest getaway in escape history.

Drina growled and cut off his path. With her finger in his face, she leaned in close. "Shall I remind you, I just re-inflated your lung, like, twenty minutes ago?"

"Aye, I was there." He grabbed the shoulder of her white lab coat and shoved her out of his way. It turned out the Reaper had a point about him not being ready to take on the world. As he pushed her out of his path, his wounds protested, and he had to brace himself not to black out.

Drina's gaze narrowed on him. Her frown deepened as she studied him, searching for signs of catastrophic organ failure.

Even if one should occur, he'd be damned if he let her know it.

"I thank ye fer yer aid, doc," he said, resuming the shuffle, "but if ye don't mind—"

"I *do* mind. You stubborn, old . . ."

Brennus stopped listening to the rant of his doctor and focused on the handsome young man all but hidden behind the wall of Phoenix. "Hello, lad. How ye bin? What brings ye to my neck of the woods?"

Jack sidestepped his boss and offered him a warm smile. "Storme was giving me a lift home when she found out you'd been hurt. Naturally, we came straight here."

Brennus liked the "naturally" part and straightened as much as his stitched ribs would allow. "Weel, since yer here, perhaps ye might keep me company while I mend. That is, unless ye have any other prior engagements?"

Jack took the invitation as intended and slid in beside him. With a supporting arm around his waist, he looked up at him. "I'm all yours. Where are we headed?"

"To bed," Drina snapped. "Doctor's orders."

Brennus let Jack see how much he agreed with his good doctor. "You heard the lady. Time to hit the horizontal."

Phoenix lifted his hands and, as usual, was far too logical.

"Aye, perhaps yer right, Egyptian," he said, considering.

"Right about what?" Drina asked. "Do I want to hear it?"

Brennus sighed and gave up the fight. "Aye, I think ye will. Phoenix pointed out how far the house is and how there are perfectly good beds, only twenty feet away."

"Well said, warrior," she said, stepping back and pointing back the way he'd come. "So, get your Humpty-Dumptied ass back to your room, and I'll even let your friend stay."

Brennus relented, said goodnight to Storme and Phoenix, and allowed Jack to help him back to bed. When his naked ass touched down on the mattress, he sent a prayer of thanks to Mr.

Sealy for his attention to detail. He also sent one to Kyrian for paying for quality.

"Can I get you anything?" Jack asked.

Brennus straightened the hem of his jonny and patted the bed. "Once ye take a load off and join me, I'll have everything I need, lad."

Jack toed off his shiny dress shoes, eased onto the mattress beside him, and rolled onto his side, so they were face-to-face. Ah, and what a lovely face it was.

"Am I keepin' ye from anything important? Honestly, I know I put ye on the spot out there. If ye need to go—"

Jack shook his head, his honey hair rustling with the movement. The lad's gaze softened, and the strain of his day seemed to drain away, leaving him looking *soooo* freaking young. "I'm right where I want to be."

Good. That was good.

Brennus closed his eyes and breathed him in. His chest inflated, and he was thankful for that. Not being able to breathe was one of his least favorite ways to suffer injury.

Not that he had a favorite.

"What happened to you?"

Brennus opened his eyes and smoothed out the line of worry across Jack's brow. "It doesnae matter. It's over, and no one was hurt too terribly bad."

"Except you. You're half-dead. Your doctor said she had to re-inflate your lung. That sounds bad to me."

Brennus started to laugh, but the pain put an end to that quickly. He wrapped his arms around his ribs and focused on breathing. "I envisioned great things for us in this bed, but I fear I'm not as able-bodied as I hoped."

Jack propped up on his elbow and looked down over him. "Don't worry about that. I'm here to keep you company, right? You can lie there and be half-dead for that."

Brennus nodded. "Perfect, then I fit the bill. I would still like to get a taste of ye. If ye don't mind doing the lion's share of the work, would ye mind maybe givin' a broken soldier a kiss to ease his suffering?"

Jack's smile was the best medicine—until he leaned in and pressed his warm, silky lips against Brennus's mouth.

That was the new best medicine.

And what a good patient he was, taking his medicine without complaint.

CHAPTER THREE

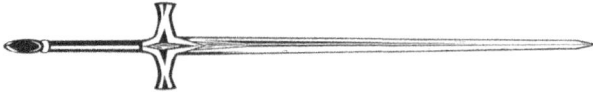

*D*anel strode across the tarmac with the bags, and handed them to the awaiting driver. Once those were taken care of, he got his girls settled in the limousine. If Sunshine were awake, he bet she'd be dazzled by the seats facing each other, and the bar and snacks and all the things Ronnie grew up with. As it was, their plus one was out cold and drooling on his mate's lapel.

"Do you want me to take her?" he asked, opening his arms.

Ronnie shook her head. "You could hold us both though."

He shifted to the bench seat beside them and pulled Ronnie and, in turn, Sunshine against his chest. "It kills me that you're suffering. If I could fix this for you, I would."

Ronnie's blonde hair brushed his chin as she nodded. It smelled like her shampoo, and it was hard to believe they had showered together before patrol only a few hours ago.

Everything had been right, life on the upswing.

It was incredible how fast things crumbled.

"I don't know how to be an orphan," she whispered, her voice weak. "I never imagined a world where I outlived my dad.

That seems crazy, now. Parents almost always die before their children, but as sick as I was, it never entered my mind."

He cupped her jaw and lifted her face to him so he could kiss her nose. "You grew up with death stalking you, baby. You fought every day to survive and won. You come from tough genes. Maybe your old man will prove everyone wrong and rally too."

He saw the tiny glimmer of hope in her eyes, and prayed he wasn't setting her up for more heartache.

But that's what humans did, wasn't it? Hope.

"I love you, Veronica Rose."

Ronnie closed her eyes and nuzzled into the crook of his neck. "I love you too, broody man."

By the time they arrived at the hospital, it was nearly seven in the morning, and the sun had risen. The driver took them to the emergency exit, parked, and came around to open the door for Ronnie.

Danel took Sunshine so she could shuffle out and when he straightened in the morning light, he looked up at the façade. It was the same hospital where he'd been with her less than a year ago, when they found out she would live, where he claimed her and got his wings.

"I, uh . . . don't know how long we'll be, Jackson," Ronnie said, unbuttoning her jacket and tossing it in the back seat.

The elderly man, dressed in a formal black suit and hat, folded his hands, and smiled down at her. "Now, don't you be worrying about that, Miss Veronica. I'm here until you're ready to leave. No question. No problem."

Ronnie squeezed his arm, and then headed inside.

Danel lived in awe of his bride. Every day, she taught him about love and life, forgiveness, and strength. She'd grown up as a southern belle in a wealthy family, and that was before her father, Howton, became a U.S. Senator.

One might expect her to be an elitist or put on airs, but his

Ronnie was as down to earth and genuine as any person could be. But at that moment, it was her strength that inspired him.

Head up, shoulders back, she strode past the media camped out on the sidewalk, and headed straight inside to the elevators.

"I hate that you know where critical care is without asking," he said, rubbing Sunshine's back as she snored softly against his neck. He was glad to have his arms full and his hands busy because being back there stirred up emotions he didn't want to think about.

When he thought Ronnie would die.

Even now, he couldn't bear to—

"Hey, broody," she said, pulling him to the side as they exited the elevator. "Don't let the past suck you in. Always looking forward, right? Never back."

He swallowed, embarrassed she was consoling him when that was his job for her. "I love you."

She winked. "I know."

Their shared chuckle lasted a fleeting second before it was back to seeking out her father. "Howton Hennington," she said to the male nurse at the desk.

The man in loose-fitting scrubs turned from updating the info on the large whiteboard and rounded the desk. "Are you family?"

Ronnie nodded. "Yes. I'm his daughter, Veronica."

The nurse—John, according to his nametag—gestured for them to follow him to one of the family rooms. "If you'll have a seat. The doctors are in with him now. I'll have them come and update you on his condition the moment they're finished."

Danel followed Ronnie into the room. She took the chair and perched herself on the edge of the seat. He laid Sunshine on the leather sofa and opened his arms. "Come here, baby. Let me hold you for a minute."

The instant response soothed his beast but broke his heart. He was a warrior, a male who fended off the evils of the world, but he had no control in this. Human frailty and death went beyond the boundaries of his powers.

And so, they waited.

~

Funny what you forget when you step out of your life for a bit . . . or a couple of centuries. As Colt hung naked from his ankles, in the bitter cold of the Ice Demon detention center, he felt the pressure of blood pulsing in his head, he smelled the frost crystalizing on his skin, he heard the haunting cries of other punishments being doled out, and he couldn't help but think of . . . *candy apples.*

When he first arrived in Toronto almost two decades ago, he was nothing more than a haughty transient. He held no expectations that a city filled with mindless sheep had anything to offer a male of his acquired tastes.

He had no intention of laying roots. He just wanted out.

Despite him excelling in Purgatory as a sexually deviant playboy and entitled asshole, he left his role as species royalty and went to the last place his family would look for him.

The Human Realm.

He was a sad sack back then. No matter how gluttonous his consumption, his longing never ceased.

He wanted. He ached. He hurt.

Nothing sated his desires.

Food didn't feed his hunger. Alcohol only brought out the vileness of his demon side. Pleasures of the flesh became tedious and hollow. He gave up on finding relief.

Then, on that first summer night, a local sporting event let out, and the sidewalks flooded with the flow of thousands of human sheep. Amazed at the volume of humans, he avoided the crush, stepped out of their path, and found himself staring at the produce of a street vendor.

In the core of downtown Toronto, manned-cart offerings abound. Salted pretzels, roasted nuts, candy floss, hot dogs. The scents draw in the humans, but the vibrant ruby red of the candy apples caught his attention.

The sweet, scarlet candy crunched beneath his fangs as the tang of the juice rushed over his tongue and down his throat. His taste buds had burst to life as the succulence coated his mouth and dripped down his chin.

Both exotic and slightly erotic, it had reminded him of the first time he'd pierced the flesh of a female and fed.

A first feeding was a monumental milestone for his people, the pairing arranged years in advance, bloodlines verified, family alliances considered. This first joining of fang to wrist was witnessed, recorded, and in the case of the royal family, lavishly celebrated.

A first feeding represented the crossing of a threshold, beginning a new phase in life, a rite of passage.

That candy apple signified the same thing. With candy stuck in his mighty canines, he'd watched the humans pass and saw their frailty, their innocence, their simple joy in wearing team jerseys and watching men fight over a ball.

He decided right then that he wanted to protect them from men like him, to preserve the human condition, so things like candy apples and sporting events lived on in a world where violence and greed so often dominated.

That was the beginning of the end for him.

That put him in league with Tanek and the Nephilim of the Toronto garrison, which created the working relationship with the Watchers, which led to the random fucking around with Brennus, which led to where he was now.

Closing his eyes, he sighed and focused on the bite of the cold, the pain in his extremities, the ache of his balls clenching so far inside his sac his throat hurt. He needed to keep the moments of poor judgment with the Celt out of his head.

They may have dabbled with the whole "sleeping with the enemy" thing, but that was reckless and would end up with either one, or both, of them dead.

No. He'd done the right thing leaving. He and Brennus had no right doing what they'd been doing. Them together was just their self-destructive sides taking advantage of their chemistry.

Apart was definitely better.

~

Layne stole a plate of fries off Collin's cook line and jogged for the elevator while the Fire Demon waved his spatula and cursed her. "Sorry," she laughed. "A girl's gotta eat."

"A girl can place an order and wait like everyone else."

"You're the best, Collin." She munched on the salty sticks of ecstasy as the old freight elevator rose to the third floor and she let herself into Zander's loft. The rumble of the bassline of the music two floors below would stop in another half hour and then her warrior would come home.

Well, not that this was their home, but it had been their love nest for the past two months. And what a love nest it was.

Closing herself in, she locked the door and headed through the dining room to the massive table the garrison had used as their war room prior to them moving to the ranch.

Part of her wondered when Zander would invite them to live in the big house with the rest of the family while another part of her understood his reluctance. Before she knew better, she'd worked for the enemy. She'd enslaved Bo. She'd allowed armed thugs to attack members of his family.

But, if Gheil and Jhaia could forgive her, she had to believe the Sumerian would too. Bo didn't mention it, but she knew how deeply he missed living as part of the Nephilim family at the ranch.

29

They'd get there. She'd prove to them and the world that she had her head on straight now. Love could do that for a girl.

Setting her plate down, she pulled the map of Toronto from the pile of research she'd been compiling and drew an ink X through the four buildings she'd checked tonight.

She'd find the Rugaru bastards that killed her nephew and when she did, her and her Viking would end them. Wheeling her mouse across the table, she opened her email, and smiled at one from Danel from earlier that night. It was a detailed account of power usage throughout the buildings of the downtown core.

Bo told her once that they weren't magicians, that finding bad guys with no leads took time and energy. She had both.

She'd find these assholes, even if it took her years.

She'd get justice for her nephew.

She'd get justice for Jhaia and their whole family.

~

Brennus stretched out in the cozy clinic recovery bed, his hand sliding over the dip in the mattress until he found the warmth of Jack's back. The room was dark, the blackout curtains pulled, the only ambiance coming from the safety light in the bathroom and the thin strip of illumination squeezing under the door. Shifting closer, he nuzzled up behind the lad and sent his hand over the soft cotton of his boxers.

Nice surprise. He missed the part where his caretaker had removed his dress clothes, but what a lovely development to wake up to. *Thank you, Lady Divinity.*

He glanced at the glowing digits hovering in the darkness beside the bed—four p.m.

Thanks to the hours of downtime, he was fully-healed, naked under a flimsy johnny, and in bed with a luscious young man who, by the scent of his arousal anytime they met, was more than interested in getting to know him better.

Reaching out with his mind, he clicked over the lock on the door and eliminated any chance of an awkward Reaper interruption.

"Jack, lad," he whispered, his voice heavy with sleep and arousal. "May I interest ye in some morning wood? My body seems to be in full working order, but I think we should test a few things out, just to make sure."

Jack's throaty chuckle preceded him, pushing back against the solid oak in question. "It's good that you're feeling better."

He splayed his fingers over Jack's abs and groaned. The guy was fit. Not warrior tank-and-tight like him, but he certainly took care of himself.

"Aye, I am. Would ye care to help me feel better still?"

Jack rolled to face him, his film star good looks and breathtaking smile the stuff of fine whiskey and wet dreams. "Let's take it slow and make sure you're healthy."

"Now, why would we do that?"

He cupped Brennus's jaw, his hands soft and gentle. "I have work to get done before the hotel opening, and last night, you were badly injured. Slow is how this is going to go."

"Patience isna one of my virtues. I'm a YOLO man, myself."

Jack laughed, threading his fingers through Brennus's long red hair. He fingered his general's braid and tugged down its length. "I'll meet you halfway. I'll help with your morning ache, and in a day or two, when you've recovered one hundred percent, you can take me out on the town, and we'll have that dinner you promised."

Brennus heard the finality in Jack's words. He also heard the anticipation. "Playin' hard to get, are ye?"

Jack lifted the hem of the johnny and pushed the fabric out of his way. His eyes caught the dim light and flashed all kinds of naughty intent. "I don't play games, and I don't take lovers on a whim. I only spend time with a man if there's a connection beyond the physical. If you're looking for an easy fuck, I'll be honest with you right now. I'm not it."

With their gazes locked, Jack took hold of his cock. The flood of pleasure after the pain of his wounds was incredible.

Brennus dropped his head back and shuddered. "Aye, I ken what yer sayin', though I'll not complain about the trade-off one bit. That feels wonderful, Jacky."

Jack chuckled and kissed him.

Brennus met his lips and groaned as the pumping rhythm started to build. Nope. No complaints at all.

~

Zander threw his body armor over his head and raised his arms for Austin to strap him in. The nightly ritual of his wife helping him ready for the streets had taken hold a few months back, and now it was part of them. It eased her to know he was heavily armed and protected. It eased him to have her care for him before facing all the ugly in the streets.

Standing pressed against his chest, she reached beneath his wings and pulled the wide straps around his waist. With the Velcro secure, she gripped the shoulder straps of the ballistics vest and pulled him forward to kiss her. "Safe home, warrior."

He pressed his lips against her forehead and breathed her deep into his lungs. His beast stretched, and his ebony wings unfurled. She was the air he breathed.

Easing back, he admired her thoroughly loved appearance: swimming in his worn t-shirt, her chestnut hair frazzled, her lips swollen from the hours of sexplay they just finished.

"With you here waiting for me, there is no other option. I love you, cowgirl. More with every breath I take." He shrugged into his Watcher vest, and then unlocked his gun closet. Once he stood fully armed and ready, he led Austin back to their bedroom.

"Be safe at the meeting, angelman. Promise me."

He understood her apprehension. The last meeting, the planning session for the Otherworld council, ended with armed thugs invading his loft and threatening the species leaders.

"I swear it, love. On my honor."

The disgruntled fussing in the adjoining room had them venturing through to the nursery.

Zander chuckled at the little hedgehog sheet tangled and twisted around her foot. She kicked, red in the face, annoyed to be held back from what she wanted. He set her free and let her claim his fist in her hands. "Did those dumb hedgehogs make you mad, sweet girl?"

Nio smiled, her feet pumping as she sucked on his silver skull ring.

"She has the patience of her father," Austin said, readying the changing table and setting out a tracksuit and tiny socks. "Does this match?"

Zander looked at the outfit. Almost all of Nio's clothes were bought by Kyrian from Burberry, Gucci, and Ralph Lauren. It was a high-end mix and match. Austin still worried that being blind, she'd dress her in something that clashed and people would be too polite to tell her the child looked goofy.

"Matches perfectly. It's the baby blue set with stars, and white socks."

She smiled and fondled the little clothing pile. "I love the feel of the cashmere ones."

Zander chuckled, reclaiming his hand and wiping his daughter's saliva on his jeans. After kissing both of his girls goodbye, he met Kyrian, Hark, and Ringo waiting for him in the foyer. "You boys ready to roll?"

His brothers were locked and loaded. The four of them

jogged down the steps to the tunnel and were buckled up in the Hummer and rolling out right on schedule.

"Thanks for asking me to come, Z," Ringo said, fiddling with the collar of his hoodie. The kid was amped, his pale whiskey-gold eyes bouncing around like a ping-pong ball. "And for the vest. It's wicked cool."

Zander had body armor custom fitted for their youngest brother. If he was out in the field with them, he'd be outfitted. "You've proven yourself part of the garrison on more than one occasion, little brother. With your transition only a month away, it's time you see what you're in for. How are your self-defense skills coming?"

Ringo shrugged and turned to Hark, sitting beside him.

The Moor smiled. "He's got good reflexes and natural instincts with defense and retreat."

Zander heard the hesitation in Hark's words. *"Buuuut?"*

"But hesitates to do harm."

All right, they could work on that. A certain level of aggression would unlock with transition. Ringo and Danel were the sons of Gabriel, and as such, less violence thrummed in their veins to begin with.

They leaned more to the cerebral side of things.

The intellect of the group.

The kid was a scribe like Danel—more accurately, he was a precog, and the closer they got to his age of transformation, the stronger his powers got. He was going to do great things.

They all agreed on that.

"Okay, listen up, little brother. You will observe, stick to the objective, and if one of us gives you an order, you follow it without hesitation, got it?"

Ringo swallowed. "Got it."

"I mean it. No questions. No fussing. If shit goes sideways, an obedient response will keep you breathing."

Ringo flipped his limp, ebony bangs out of his eyes and met his gaze. "I'll lapdog it like you read about, Z."

Zander laughed, though his chest was still tight as hell.

"Don't worry. For reals. I got this."

"Yeah, you do." Hark met Ringo for a knuckle bump, and both made an explosion noise and flopped back in their seats.

Zander chuckled. Hark was a man of few words and little emotion. Their kid brother had worked his magic on all of them. His bowels twisted as he pulled into the parking lot of the sanitarium and cut the meaty rumble of the truck.

Had he made the right call bringing Ringo into this mess? Daemons were daemons by nature. Could they be reasoned with? *Sweet Lady, please protect our little man tonight. And if I made the wrong call, let me pay the price, not him.*

Grabbing the door handle, he pulled the lever and dropped out into the chill of the night. "All right boys, right and tight."

CHAPTER FOUR

*C*olt stepped into the lobby of his condo building and nodded to the concierge standing like one of the Queen's guards at his station in the corner. Decked out in a stiffly pressed red jacket with gold and black trim, and the little red monkey hat to boot, no one would ever guess that aside from him looking like he was a shoo-in for a part in The Nutcracker, he was a Crossroads Demon on the hunt of humans desperate to change their course.

"Hey, Martin. How's things?"

The two of them often shot the shit about the other tenants and what the guy witnessed on the street. He was a bit of a run on chatty-Cathy, but it never hurt to have another set of eyes and ears on the home front.

"Good."

When nothing else followed the clipped answer, he tried again. "How's Lucy. Has she seen the light and kicked your sorry ass to the curb yet?"

"Nope."

Were they playing some one-word game he didn't know about? "Did I miss something?"

"Nope."

"*Riiiiight.* I can tell. S'all good in the hood, eh?"

"Brar'don, there you are."

Colt cursed and dropped his bag from his shoulder.

Suddenly the attitude made sense. Martin had learned the easygoing daemon cop was Ice Demon royalty. That always tripped things up. With a sigh, he resigned himself.

There was only one person in Toronto who called him by his given name, and that was his PITA cousin.

"Your Majesty," he said, turning to the king of his species.

Andz'gar looked him over and frowned. Natch. "What the hell have you done to yourself?"

Colt raised his fingers to his mouth and yawned. "To what do I owe the honor of your house call . . . and what's it going to take to make it end?"

Andz'gar signaled for his two loyal lapdogs in suits to drop back to the glass doors. "You disappeared almost two months ago without a word, and with no explanation. Whether you recognize it or not, you *are* one of my subjects, and I have every right to demand answers."

Colt scowled. "I don't report to you, Andy. My comings and goings are nobody's business but my own."

Andz'gar's jaw tightened, and he leaned close. His dark and rugged looks enhanced as his eyes glowed turquoise. "First, I am your king, and you should address me as such. If I didn't think you'd enjoy it, I'd string you up and have you flayed for insulting me with that childish human name. Second, your well-being becomes my business when I get calls and visits from your Watcher pets, wondering where you are. Do you think I want them tracking me down?"

No. He supposed not.

With the Red-Metal Rebellion in full swing, all eyes were locked on the Darkworld leaders gauging who was with the cause and who wasn't.

Andz'gar sat so firmly perched on the fence, the points of the pickets were rammed up his ass. Waiting to see who comes out on top was a weak stance, but that's what you got from a pampered aristocrat who hadn't spent a day in the trenches.

"I'll let Zander know all is well. Despite what you think, they're good guys trying to correct Otherworld injustices. The rebellion is only getting people killed."

Andz'gar tugged the cuffs of his black dress shirt and righted his perfect sleeves. "Well, they almost got me killed."

Colt rolled his eyes. The attack in Zander's loft had been a test of strength, nothing more than a show. Andz'gar walked out of that Otherworld Council planning session with a chip on his shoulder and more shit to sling.

"Anything else? Keep Zander out of your hair, *annnnd?*"

"Why did you submit yourself for conditioning?"

There it is. Fucking hell. Did his cousin get reports on what everyone did in Purgatory, or was he part of a special club? Okay, time to end this. Colt pushed back on his urge to remind Andz'gar who had the goods when it came down to a one on one. "Like you said, I like it rough and painful. Couldn't get what I needed here, so I headed home for a little spa treat."

"Reconditioning as a treat?" Andz'gar shook his head. "Not even a sick bastard like you subjects himself to the five phases for anything less than a cataclysmic event."

Not going there. Nope. Not opening that door.

"Sorry to disappoint, Andy," he said, crossing his arms. "There's nothing to tell. There's no crime in a sadist getting off on his own terms—especially a depraved daemon like me. You should embrace your dark and distasteful sometime. Who knows, you might discover something about yourself." He looked him over and frowned. "Or maybe not. Whatevs."

"Deflect all you want, Brar'don, but if you're a danger to yourself or our people, I'll find out, and I *will* take care of it."

"You do you, Andy." Bending to the floor, Colt grabbed the

handles of his duffle and slung it over his shoulder. "Now, if you'll excuse me, I need to go unpack, water my plants, feed my cat . . . you know, *soooo* much to catch up on."

He rounded the corner and called for an elevator. Despite a minor case of the shakes, the good news was his daemon side held strong. Not one indicator he'd been in trouble. Not one sign of that nasty cataclysmic event Andz'gar suspected.

Yee-fucking-haw, he was cured.

~

Zander bowed his head to the Serpentine females awaiting them at the entrance of their sanitarium home. They were a slim, wiry species by nature but thankfully, with his efforts, they were starting to fill out and held a bit of color in their cheeks. "Thank you for seeing us, ladies. I swear, we mean you and yours no harm. We'll say what we came to say and leave you in peace."

"Leave us in peace or in pieces?" a young male said, glaring at them from inside the entranceway.

Zander straightened, not at all surprised by the hostility. They had, after all, slaughtered every grown male of their species over the past six months. "You must be Garrard."

The kid jutted out his chin. "Why do you want to know?"

Zander made an easy gesture toward the open door. "How about you invite us in, and we discuss it. I've spoken to your queens and I assure you, there is nothing nefarious about our visit. We simply wish to talk."

The females said nothing. They watched the boy, waiting for his reply. Yep, this was Garrard, the oldest male left of the Serpentines and the one he needed to get through to if they wanted to change the course of the future.

"Please, son. Twenty minutes of your time. It's important to your people."

~

Danel stood at the long window of Howton's hospital room and stared at the city of Atlanta sprawling out toward the rose-colored horizon. Four. There were four times in his life he'd felt truly helpless: as a boy in the clutches of violent men, when a Shedim Demon severed his dagger hand and he lost his place in the garrison, when he learned Ronnie would die from a rare and cruel disease . . . and now, smelling her heart-shattering grief as she said goodbye to her father.

The tests were run. The dye was cast.

Howton wouldn't come back from this.

The door to the bathroom whispered open, and his baby girl toddled out. Technically, Sunshine wasn't theirs yet, but he pitied anyone who tried to separate them. Her bright blue eyes and bouncing blonde curls stole his heart each and every time he laid eyes on her.

"Hey monkey, everything okay?"

She came to him, and he picked her up so they could look out the window together. With both of her little hands, she cupped his ear. "Ronnie cries for her daddy like I cries for my mommy."

He blinked at the sting in his eyes and hugged her tighter. "I know, baby. Losing someone you love hurts."

"Is that why you crying?" Her palm swept away his tears, and she leaned in close to look at him. With her forehead pressed against his, her two eyes became one. "You sad too?"

Danel was raised to be a tough guy, to eat his emotions, to play the part of the heartless soldier. That was a bullshit path to anger and hostility. Ronnie taught him differently. Own your pain. Speak your truths. Live a genuine life.

"It hurts me when my two favorite girls hurt. I want to help you, and I can't make it better."

Sunshine hugged him tight around the neck and squeezed. "Mommy says hugs make everything better."

He held on tight and breathed in the little girl's concern. She was worried for him? "I love you, Sunshine."

She leaned back in his arms and pressed her palms on his cheeks. Her eyes twinkled under the fluorescent lights as her smile beamed with the radiance and warmth of a summer's day. "I luvs you too, silly."

"Can I get in on this action?" Ronnie said, joining them.

Danel pulled her in and kissed the top of her head. "I think there's enough love to go around."

Ronnie sagged against him, and he realized Sunshine was right. Hugs did make things better. Too soon, his beloved mate straightened and pulled away. "Let's go. It could be hours or days, but they don't think he'll ever wake up. I've said what I needed to say."

Danel kissed her temple, and set Sunshine on her feet. "Go pack up your toys, monkey."

With his arms free, he pulled Ronnie in tight and breathed deep. Her fall-apart was close, building in the foreground, but she reeled it in. "I wish there were something I could do."

"There is," she said, tightening her grip at his back. "After we get home and eat, I'll take a hot bath, and then my husband will make endless love to me until I'm so exhausted, I fall more unconscious than asleep."

Over her shoulder, he studied Howton's still form and felt the ache of how fleeting life and love could be. One moment, a strong-as-an-ox, stubborn, U.S. Senator, the next . . . a man taken by death.

If Ronnie wanted to be worshipped until she passed out, he was *soooo* on board with that. "All right, let's get you two fed and to bed."

∽

Brennus finished patrolling the Lakeshore with Phoenix and Bo, and they headed uptown toward Zander's club. They still had an hour before they needed to be at the O-Zone for the Otherworld Council meeting. Even if they crawled, they'd be there in a quarter of that. Whistling a jaunty tune, he distracted himself with the consideration of where to take Jack tomorrow evening for their dinner date.

If the lad's sample of affection at the clinic earlier stood the indicator of future pleasures, he would happily accept the challenge of wooing the man for more.

"Wipe that grin off, Celt," Seth said, pointing to his face. "You're freaking me out. Head in the game."

Brennus hiked his leathers, and pulled his vest forward to cover what was happening behind his fly. He'd spent centuries going hard and hot with nameless, faceless males, and never explored the idea of a relationship.

Though locking down with one person and lifing it like his mated brothers held no interest, the idea of someone familiar in his bed when he got home each morning held an appeal.

"Seriously, you two," Seth said, waving a finger between him and Bo. "Between your walking hard-on, whistling, and Bo sexting Layne every other minute, we might as well be out here with a sign hanging off our dicks saying, 'Horny and distracted. Take your best shot.'"

Brennus rolled his eyes and chuffed. "Yer a fine one to talk, Egyptian. Four months ago, yer mind and mouth were filled with nothin' but Thea and yer son."

"And you told me to get my head out of my ass and pay attention. Great sex and someone to love does us no good if we get sloppy on the streets and wind up with a red metal slug spreading our gray matter."

He couldn't argue that point.

"Fine. Consider me cock-blocked and fully on duty."

His phone vibrated in his pocket at the same time Seth and

Bo checked theirs. It was a group message from Colt. *Back in the land of the living. Call off the search.*

Call off the search?

Really? After two months?

Brennus's beast paced within. He didn't know whether to be relieved or pissed. He opted for the latter. "Listen lad, I've got something to check on. I'll meet ye at the club in plenty of time." With that, he jogged into the darkness of the shadows and threw his molecules into the night sky.

~

Fresh from the shower, Colt dressed in blue jeans and a gray long-sleeve shirt to hide the red welts and bruising of his skin. Self-induced punishment wouldn't raise an eyebrow with daemons, but well-meaning humans were a different story. With his gun holster strapped on and his firearm loaded, he felt ready to face the world. He hit send on the group text, knowing what would come next. He'd taken the coward's out two months ago, and now he needed to man up.

Leaving the glass door to his balcony open an inch, he pulled two glasses from the bar and started pouring.

"Call off the *search?*" the rough brogue snapped behind him, and he steeled himself against the coming storm. "Are ye feckin' kiddin' me? I've been out of my heed fer weeks. Did I kill ye? Do ye suffer somewhere from my blood poisoning yer body. Have ye any idea how I worried for ye?"

Colt turned to face the wrath of the Celt, drink in hand. He held it out, but Brennus's hands were locked in white-knuckled fists at his side. "I'm sorry, General. Honestly. It was a dick move to leave without a word. Give me everything you've got. I deserve it."

The warrior's pupils flared, and Colt fought the urge to follow the cue down that road. He knew what Brennus wanted to give him, what had become their fallback when emotions ran hot. It couldn't happen that way again.

Not ever again.

"I went to Purgatory to take care of a problem. I did that. I'm back. End of story."

A rush of cold air hit as Brennus stormed forward. The warrior's right hook cracked his cheek like an anvil. Knocked off his feet, the glasses of whiskey flew from his hands and smashed on the floor. Colt's vision snapped like a live wire in his head as blood warmed his mouth.

Unbidden, his fangs dropped as his cock grew hard. Daemon foreplay was not in the cards for them. Rolling to his palms, Colt pushed to his feet and faced his disgruntled lover.

Fuck, the guy was a vision of fury, his flaming red hair and gold eyes both wild. He was a beast. A breathtaking, powerful beast of passion. "I did what I needed in order to survive. I know you don't understand that, but what you and I did"—he gestured to the space between them—"can't happen again. It's dangerous for both of us."

The tension in his mighty warrior eased a touch, and he cursed. "I understand survival, cop. Ye shoulda just told me ye needed it to end. I'm a feckin' grown male, not a schoolgirl crush. I thought I killed ye. That wasnae fair nor deserved."

Colt played the whole thing wrong. He owned that. He hadn't told Brennus the truth because, in that state, he wouldn't have had the strength to walk away.

If he hadn't, things would've been a thousand times worse.

Colt eyed the broken glass on the floor and went straight to the bottle. Pressing his lips to the mouth of the bottle, he swigged back three big gulps. "I'll apologize as many times as you need to hear the words. It wasn't cool. You didn't deserve to suffer because of it, you're right. I fucked up. I regret it."

Brennus checked his watch and cursed. "I gotta bounce."

That was a relief, actually. Colt nodded and set the bottle on the coffee table. "'Kay, you go do your thing."

"So, that's that," Brennus said, walking back to the open patio door and pegging him with a sad glance. "It was fun while it lasted, cop."

It was. The two of them were hot and combustible. "Just know that I didn't leave you hanging because I didn't care—"

Brennus's form dissolved and disappeared.

Colt swigged back another gulp of booze and let the alcohol sting his split lip. "It was because I cared too much."

CHAPTER FIVE

*Z*ander's new blue Hummer rumbled into the parking lot of the club with Ringo riding shotgun, and Garrard, his mother, and two bodyguards in the back. Fuck, the thing was a beast. If he'd known how much he would love owning a tricked-out tank, he would've bought one years ago. Turning the keys, the world fell woefully quiet—until he opened his door, and the pounding thrum of the music inside his club filled the air.

"I know this place, Sumerian," one of the bodyguards said. "It is not suitable to bring Master Garrard or milady within."

He glanced back at the male who spoke and then to the boy who looked more intrigued than annoyed. Zander pointed to the metal stairs leading to the side door. "We'll be meeting upstairs in my private space. We won't be going into the club proper nor running into any of the patrons."

As he escorted the group, Ringo did as instructed, chatting it up with the pre-pubescent Serpentine Master. Teen to teen, the two whispered back and forth, their conversation growing easier by the moment.

"No way," Garrard hissed.

Zander chuckled. By the raised eyebrows and Ringo's exaggerated nod, the boys were discussing the highlights of O-Zone being a hedonist club.

Fighting to appear serious, he thought back to Ringo's reaction when their little brother first arrived almost two years ago. When nobody was looking, the kid got drunk, stripped down, and performed a full dance number in one of the go-go cages. Meck, his head bouncer, captured the whole event on video and sent it to him. He, in turn, sent it to all his brothers.

You never know when you're gonna need a piss-your-pants laugh to cheer you up.

"Watcher?"

Zander blinked back to the present and punched in the door code. "My apologies, milady. Follow me. The others will arrive shortly, and the meeting will begin."

∾

Danel helped Jackson unload the bags from the trunk, but when he tried to carry them inside, his good intentions were met with a bit of a panic. The guy looked like Danel kicked his puppy. He never grew up with servants—he *was* the servant in the ages long past—but in this case, he could allow the man to do his job. "Thank you, Jackson. Your help is much appreciated."

Ronnie's knowing smile made his cheeks flush hot. "What? I needed to lend a hand after a long day."

Ronnie side-hugged him and turned toward the entrance of the sprawling Georgia estate. "You could bench-press Jackson, all the bags, and carry Sunshine in one arm. You're my hero, broody, whether you carry the suitcases or not."

"Angel, come see the pretty flowers!"

Danel winced as Sunshine's excited call seemed to echo across all of Atlanta. He met her up the walkway and bent to see what had captured her attention. "Yeah, those are beautiful.

Maybe tomorrow, you can pick two or three and put them in a vase for your room."

Sunshine shoved her face into the flower and came back with yellow pollen on her nose.

"Monkey, can you do me a big favor?"

Sunshine tilted her head, her blonde locks hanging close to touching the rainbow of tulips lining the walk. "Acourse."

He brushed her nose clean and cupped the round of her cheek. "You know how you see my wings and know that I'm part-angel?"

"Uh-huh."

"Not everyone can see them. You can, because you are *soooo* incredibly special, but me being an angel is a secret that I'm not supposed to share. Do you understand?"

"And Bo and Seth and Z too?"

"Right. We're in a secret club and are supposed to seem like ordinary people on the streets."

"But yous angels." Her crinkled nose was hands down the cutest thing he'd ever seen. Goddess, if he could preserve these moments with her forever, he'd live and die a happy man.

"Yes, but that's our secret. Do you understand?"

"No."

Ronnie giggled and squatted down beside them. "You know how we watched *Spiderman* a couple of nights ago?"

"The funny boy on the string?"

Ronnie nodded. "You know how he keeps his red suit in his backpack and only told his best friend that he went out at night and fought bad men?"

"Uh-huh."

"Danel and Zander and Bo . . . their secret is like that."

"Buts we gets to know?"

Ronnie smiled. "Because we're super special."

Sunshine's face grew serious, and then she frowned. "Buts I like calling you Angel."

Danel winked and squeezed her shoulder. "You can call me Angel when it's just us, but when there are other people around, maybe call me Danel, or my brothers call me D. You could call me that."

Her eyes widened as her smile lit up. "I'll call you Kitty. Ronnie says Kitty is a good name and he won't mind." She nodded her head and grasped his fingers. "Come on, Kitty."

Danel groaned and Ronnie burst out laughing. Given the situation, if it brought his wife joy, Sunshine could call him whatever she wanted. "Much better. Kitty, it is."

～

Brennus stood from his vantage point on the roof of the club and watched Zander and Ringo escort the young Serpentine leader inside. "Nicely done, boss," he said into their comm system. "I admit it. I was skeptical the Serpentines would attend after what's happened. Yer breaking ground, Z. Good luck."

He hadn't expected an answer and wasn't surprised when the comm line remained silent. Maybe this Otherworld Council might work. Listen to the grievances. Fix what they could. Fewer daemons to kill. Fewer enemies trying to kill them.

What did a Nephilim warrior do in a time of peace?

He had no idea. There had never been one.

"The Dragons are here," Hark said from the rooftop across the street. Two stories higher, the Moor had a line of sight to the club roof access and the side door.

Rayvn and Wilder dropped out of an orange-and-black Harley Davidson Limited Edition pickup. The two had their guard up and sensed them immediately. They nodded first to Hark and then to him.

There would not be a repeat performance after the fiasco of the last meeting. Luckily, when Bo allowed the enemy to storm the walls, the room was filled almost exclusively with friends, family, and those loyal to Zander's new world order.

Tonight would be different. They needed this meeting to go smoothly.

"Cassi, Dougal, and the Greek," Hark reported.

"How's it looking, my brothers?" Kyrian asked, in his ear.

"Downright boring," Brennus said.

"Good." Kyrian opened the door for his mate and offered her a hand. "Boring is right where I want things. Let's keep it that way."

"Your wish is our command, Greek." Brennus scanned the skyline, the rooftops, and the streets in all four directions.

Things looked quiet.

Almost too quiet.

~

Colt finished with his captain at the station and stood on the stoop outside the precinct. The hurt and anger in Brennus's eyes hollowed him out. Being a daemon of the Hell Realm didn't excuse willfully hurting a friend. Or even a friend-with-bene-fits. The ache in his chest was foreign. Since when did he do guilt? Oh, since he crossed every line with the enemy and the universe fucked him for it. Oh, right.

"Hey, Creed, you back?"

Colt lifted his chin to fellow Staff Sergeant, John Blakney, smoking on the steps. "Yep. Back next week."

"Good. You were missed."

"Yeah," one of his constables added, escorting a drunk inside. "Only because you got his straight graveyard."

Colt laughed and headed down the steps to the parking lot. "Tough it out for a few more shifts, boys. Then I'll save your asses and retake the night." Kicking his leg over the seat of his Ducati, he sat down, and pulled on his helmet.

May in Toronto was early in the season for motorcycles but after weeks in the freezer section of Purgatory, it felt downright balmy on the streets. Gripping the throttle, he gunned it, and headed for O-Zone.

The Otherworld Council meeting would wrap soon, and he wanted to explain to Z in person why Andz'gar wasn't there. He wasn't sure if he was going to lead with his cousin being weak and shortsighted, or a spiteful idiot.

Ice Demons, because of their fallen angel origins, possessed temperaments closer to peacekeepers than other daemon species. He didn't understand why Andz'gar waffled so much over the idea of supporting the Nephilim in their bid for Otherworld reform.

The guy seemed to be stuck in a cycle of violence that offered no one anything.

The parking lot at the club was packed as he pulled up, so he parked in the shadows around back and shut things down. The building diffused the deep base of the music inside but the beat was still audible and easy to follow.

With quiet ordinances in the city after 11 p.m., he had to wonder what kind of warding Zander had on the building to keep the humans from hearing it and complaining. As he pondered that, he reached into his pocket and pulled out a stick of pure cigarette bliss.

Estrangement to his home over the past few decades forced him to downgrade to human cigarettes. One of the side benefits of spending time down in Purgatory—the only bene-fit, really—was him reestablishing a supplier of Darkworld smoke.

Haze was a beautiful thing.

He flicked his lighter and drew a long pull.

Teasing tendrils of happy-happy-feel-good fluttered their way through his system. Sweet Prince, he forgot what a trip it was to simply let go. Haze didn't induce anything harmful or dangerous, it simply blocked all synaptic signals that dealt with anger, guilt, and heartache.

The daemon trifecta.

In an instant, he felt a thousand times lighter.

He pulled another lungful and wrapped himself tighter in the warm and fuzzy of life. Cool. *Soooo* cool.

"Aye, Jack, it's me."

Colt cursed, covered the glow of his heater, and checked that he was fully engulfed in the shadows.

Brennus sat his ass on the loading dock of the club, his long, muscular legs swinging, his phone propped at his ear. "What time can ye get away tomorrow night, lad?" He paused for a moment. "Uh-huh . . . All right, I'll swing by the hotel at eight, and we'll get that dinner."

Colt's body roared with heat while his brain roared with fury. Only hours after he'd extinguished their fire, the Celt was on the make? Son of a bitch.

Brennus laughed at something the pretty-boy man-child said. "Aye, after experiencing your talents earlier, I moved you to the top of my to-do list." More of that fucking laughter. "A kilt? Of course, why . . . all right, you're on. Tomorrow then. Sweet dreams, Jacky."

Colt pinched off the glowing ember of his cigarette and cursed the loss of his momentary bliss.

No amount of Haze would ease him now.

~

Zander praised Thea for a job well done and led the Serpentine entourage out of his loft and back down to the Hummer. The first, official, Otherworld Council meeting had a few glitches and personality clashes, but overall, things went well. He was pleased and thought they had a solid foundation to build upon moving forward.

"Garrard, I realize there is a lot of bad blood between Serpentines and Nephilim right now, but, as you grow into your rule, try to keep things in perspective. Up until the past two years, we had no issues with your people unless they violated the laws."

"And then you killed everyone."

Zander glanced into the rearview and met the kid's gaze. "Gregor joined the Red-Metal Rebellion and came after us, son. His son then came after us and kidnapped my sister-in-law and my nephew. Coming after us is what killed the males of your species. Neither of us wants that to keep happening, do we?"

The boy stared at him, his eyes a normal ruby red and not the sunken pits of his elders. "No, but many of the females are very angry."

He nodded and changed lanes. "They have every right to be angry. What happened was a tragedy, and it left them in a difficult position with a tough life ahead. That's why I've tried to help. I bought that sanitarium and signed it over to your elders. My other sister-in-law, the Mistress of Shedim you met tonight, is arranging regular food distribution for your community. We'll work together for a better future."

The boy looked to Ringo. "What do you think?"

Ringo shrugged. "This war sucks. Z wants to help feed your people and keep them in a home where they're safe. I think a great leader would do that and forget about revenge and repeating the mistakes of the males who ruled before you. Be your own Master, dude. Then you'll be a hero."

"That's a simplistic viewpoint, young Watcher," the queen said. "Garrard has many pressures and opinions to consider. To simply wash away the past might not be possible."

"Why not?"

"Ringo, manners." Zander narrowed his gaze on his brother and hoped the kid got the picture. They were making inroads here, not alienating the mother of the boy they needed on their side.

"With respect, milady," Ringo said, softening his tone, "why isn't it that simple? Attacking my brothers resulted in getting your men killed. Zander and the others want to end killing and work for a better future. Your females want a better future. The Otherworld Council gives you a place to fight for your rights. Other than revenge, why wouldn't you at least try?"

Out of the mouths of babes, Zander thought.

Yep. Ringo was one hell of an asset to the garrison.

~

Danel left his beautiful Ronnie soaking in a hot bath and went to check on Sunshine. If the little monkey got lost, it would take him all night to find her. Not that he needed to worry. The Hennington home might be a mansion, but love and warmth radiated from every piece of furniture and every picture hanging on the wall. He gave Howton huge props for that.

After Ronnie's sister, Clara, died, and her mother, Scarlett, was killed in a car bombing, he could've withdrawn and lost sight of his remaining daughter. He hadn't. He'd been the rock Ronnie depended on all through her illness and her life.

The squealing delight of his girl in a fit of giggles drew him across the hall. Aibileen had doted on her all through dinner and dessert. More like Ronnie's surrogate mother than a cook and head of household, that woman was a saint.

A saint who was a fabulous cook.

"What's so funny in here," he said, stepping in to join the fun. Inside the doorway, he stopped dead in his tracks. His wings flared and his Mark burst gold. "Who the fuck are you, and what are you doing?"

The man sitting on the floor with Sunshine wore a starched white shirt and a confident smile behind tortoise shell glasses.

Perfectly groomed, his fine, flaxen hair curled over his ears, not a strand out of place. Education and breeding bled out of his pours and Danel despised him immediately.

Sunshine squealed as he scooped her into his arms and eyed her up and down. Despite the raging of his beast, she seemed fine, her eyes sparkling as always.

He turned to the stranger, thinking the asshole might live through the night after all. "I asked you a question, Ivy League. Who the fuck are you, and what are you doing up here?"

His brow arched, his smile coy and smug. "So, you're the husband. Howton mentioned you were over-the-top possessive. I'm surprised Nica puts up with it."

Nica . . . as in Ver*onica*?

Danel suddenly needed his hands free to frog-march this smarmy asshole downstairs and wring his neck. Kissing Sunshine's cheek, he set her on the bed with her zoo puzzle book. "You get started on the zebra, sweet girl. I'll be right back to make the animal noises for you."

"Okay, Kitty," she said, screwing up her face in the most hilarious attempt at a wink he'd ever seen.

He laughed despite himself and winked back at her. Turning to the intruder, he pointed to the hall. "After you."

Mr. Armani had the good sense to get moving. "All this hostility is unnecessary. I assure you, I am as welcome in this home as you are. I merely came by to collect a few files off of Howton's desk. Despite his current condition, there are time-sensitive business matters to address."

They hit the top of the stairs, and Ivy League turned and extended a smooth-skinned palm. "Bentley Walker, solicitor for the Hennington family."

Danel ignored the proffered digits and pointed down to the main floor. "Howton's office is on the main floor. If this was a late-night professional call, you could've gathered what you needed and left without disturbing anyone. The fact that you intruded into our private quarters suggests there's more to it. So, what's your deal?"

The solicitor laid a casual hand on the railing and turned to descend to the main floor. "You sound more than a little paranoid. Honestly, whatever my business or affairs with Nica might be, they are our own."

Danel didn't appreciate the way he used the word "affairs" but didn't take the bait. Whatever this asshole thought he had going on with Ronnie, he was mistaken. Danel escorted him to the door and put out his hand.

Bentley picked up a leather, monogrammed briefcase from the sideboard and arched that manicured brow once more. "Am I to guess what you want?"

Danel smiled. "I want your key, motherfucker. If you work for the family, you can ring the bell and be announced like everyone else. Skulking into a little girl's rooms at night is not only creepy, it's dangerous. A paranoid male like me is liable to snap a neck first and ask questions later."

After a moment of consideration, Mr. Spit-and-polish reached into the pocket of his designer slacks and pulled out a gold key ring. Twisting one of the keys free, he placed it on the marble top of the sideboard and shook his head. "Veronica and I have history. She might be slumming it now, but a lady of her stature doesn't turn her back on things for long. Please tell her I dropped in to check on her."

Danel snorted. "Yeah, I'll do that."

With the trash taken out, he locked the door, shut off the lights, and jogged up the grand staircase two at a time. Sunshine was back to giggling again, and he had to laugh. She was such a bundle of happiness. She wasn't in her room, so he followed her voice further down the hall. Rounding the doorjamb to the upstairs parlor, he stopped dead in his tracks for the second time in ten minutes.

"Yeah, okay, so that happened."

CHAPTER SIX

*C*olt was in hell—not literally this time—but still, the torture was real, and he ate up the burn. As he sat on his bike down a dark side street across from the soon-to-be open Queen Hotel, he watched Brennus escort his date to his R8. Fucking, pansy-assed, Nancy-boy human. He'd never gotten a ride in the Celt's car. It stoked more than a pang of jealousy that he never would.

That car stirred a serious hard-on.

He finished his third bottle of high-gravity hooch, and studied the Celt, decked out and dressed to impress in his kilt and shitkickers.

Yep, serious hard-on.

He opened bottle four of liquid mind-numbification and shifted his stance to ease some of the tension pushing at his fly. This pain and suffering would end. He took the high road and broke it off. Good guys won, right?

Yep. Brennus was off the menu. Outta bounds. Forbidden fruit. Verboten, and all that. Geez, as a sadist, he really hit a home run on this one.

Yay me!

The teenager on Brennus's arm must have said something funny because the warrior tossed back his head and barked a laugh. The night breeze caught the fucker's hair, and it fanned out around his face like a fiery, red mane.

Sweet Prince, did he know how hot he was?

He watched Brennus continue to flirt, and cursed. Yeah, he was well aware of how hot he was and used it to full advantage.

Asshole.

I'm a feckin' grown male not a schoolgirl crush.

Obvi. Colt kicked himself for catching a case of the feels and cursed his overestimation of his effect on the warrior.

Lesson learned. Still, he doubted that baby-faced human would ever call out the beast that lived within the Celt. He'd seen that side of Brennus on a small scale during their lewd interludes, and it was a heady, powerful thing.

He wished he had the chance to go full beast with the guy.

"So, it's true." Andz'gar stepped off the curb and blocked his view. As if, for some reason, he'd rather look at his cousin primped in a couple grand worth of labels and be impressed. *Not.* "When one of my staff told me you were fraternizing with a Watcher on a personal level, I stuck a blade through his throat for suggesting a thing so vile."

Colt rolled his eyes, his boozy evening making everything about this seem oddly absurd. "Ten thoooousand bucks says you didn't stick a blade through his throat. You either lied about that or had one of your ass-lickers do it for you."

Andz'gar slapped him across the mouth, hard and sharp. "How dare you disrespect your king."

Colt laughed and licked the blood that seeped from the lip Brennus split last night. "You hit like a girl, Andy. For fuck's sake, close your fist and at least try to be a man once in a while."

The next strike knocked him and his bike over. The spinny centrifuge of the alley was a Mr. Toad's Wild Ride moment, even though the footpeg tearing into his leg hurt like a mofo. "That's the spirit, Andy. Keep that up, and you might grow a pair one of these days."

Andz'gar circled the front tire and glared down at him. "You're a disgrace to our kind, Brar'don."

Colt laughed harder. "Honestly, that *you* can even say that with a straight face is funnier than you'll ever understand."

"Really? I never fucked a Watcher."

Colt fought to keep his head up. It felt like it weighed a million pounds. "Don't knock it 'till you should try it. You might learn a few things. Except no, the only one that fucks males is Ice Demon'ed out, I'm afraid. Been there, had that, you'd never measure up."

Andz'gar kicked him square in the forehead. His head snapped back and cracked against the asphalt. "Is this why you pressured me to join the Otherworld Council? Did your filthy lover use you to leverage Ice Demons to their side?"

Colt let gravity take hold and starfished on the asphalt. "No, Andy. I was trying to help you make a smart choice for once. Zander will revolutionize the Otherworld. That you don't see that looks bad on all of us."

"You. Help. Me? Pathetic. You sneak around, fucking a Watcher assassin, and lecture me on smart choices?"

"Hey, give me a break. I broke it off." Colt raised his finger and pointed at the center Andz'gar of the blurry images of his cousin hovering over him. "I submitted myself for reconditioning, and got reset. I deserve some credit."

Andz'gar frowned. "I'm done, Brar'don. That your filthy affair came to reconditioning proves how skewed your judgment has become. You dote on the humans like their lives matter. You drop your pants and bend over for our enemy. Don't you see that this realm polluted you? As your king, it's my duty to put things right and restore honor to our species."

"Uh-huh," Colt said, no longer tracking. After a while of

listening to Andz'gar, everything started to sound like the teacher in the *Peanuts* cartoons—*Whawa wawawawa.*

Colt closed his eyes and rested his cheek on the pavement. The cold soothed the nausea swirling in his gut, and calmed the thundering rush in his ears. When he opened things up again, he was alone.

Good. Alone was good.

After struggling out from under his bike, he got things righted and thought about swinging up and over the seat. He was in no shape to ride, and Brennus and his human were gone. Tracking them would be skeevy anyway.

Ass-planting against the wall, he decided to sleep it off. Fucking Andz'gar. Didn't his cousin see his sacrifice?

He'd given up the Celt for him, for his rule, for his people.

If things kept on with Brennus, sure as shit, he would pull the arm of the Ice Demon slot machine and be gold-barring it all the way to Hell and back.

No. Thank. You.

~

Brennus stared across the candlelit table and wondered what the hell he was doing wooing a human. And not just any human, Storme's PA and right-hand man. This was a bad idea on so many levels. Yesterday afternoon, he'd woken up with the lad and had been gung-ho. Tonight, the conversation was stellar, the male looked and smelled divine, and he didn't see it going anywhere.

Since when did he want it to go somewhere?

What changed?

The answer was more a who than a what. Colton Creed.

Colt came home last night, and whatever went on in the past weeks, the guy wasn't all right. He was fronting like a pro, but Brennus's gift from the Choir was Otherworld energy.

Colt's mojo was *waaaay* off.

He was hurting, and as shitty as it was to be dumped before they were even a thing, there was more to this.

"Am I boring you?" Jack said, his mouth curved up at one side. "I've been told that I'm good company, yet your mind is definitely not here with me. So, who is it with?"

Brennus looked at the young man and sighed. "No, ye don't bore me, Jack. Yer handsome and smart and I enjoy yer company verra much. But yer right, my mind is somewhere else. A male I care about blew me off, and I thought that was the end of it, but he showed up last night, and . . ."

"*Annnnd* now you're wondering?"

Brennus sat back and frowned. "I'm sorry. Ye warned me that ye needed more than a physical tryst with a man, and I respect ye too much to lie to ye."

Jack picked up his wine and finished his drink. When he set the glass down on the table, he turned it a few times on the tablecloth before looking up. His smile went a long way in easing Brennus's guilt.

"Honesty means more to me than guilty pleasures any day of the week, Celt. I told you from the beginning, I'm new here and want to get the lay of the land. I'd consider myself lucky to keep you as a friend. That you're tied up right now, is bad timing, but I hope we'll have more dinners and other chances to explore the city together."

Brennus tossed a couple of hundreds on the table and exhaled the tension in his chest. "Yer a gracious man, Jack. I'd like that verra much. And yes, once I get myself sorted, there's a fabulous steakhouse I want to take ye to, and a Korean barbeque place too."

Jack stood and set his linen napkin on the table next to his plate. "I look forward to it."

~

Storme stood in the lobby of her hotel and twirled like a little girl while her hubby chuckled. "We did it. On time. On budget. By the opening gala next week, this place will be perfect. And I did it all without Cleo Queen and her back-up band of suits and sneers. Suck it, Mr. Logan."

Is that human still bothering you? Phoenix asked across the telepathic link they shared.

As much as Jim Logan annoyed her, he didn't deserve to have an angry Dark Angel beating down his door. "No, tough guy, I laid it out for him, and he'll get used to the new normal. From now on, my only partner is my dear, wonderful hubby. Can you believe it came together so well?"

Of course it did. He caught her up in his arms and swung her around once more. Her shoe flung across the polished tile of the lobby and they laughed. *You've always been the talent behind Queen Hotels, not my bitch mother. She made you feel like you needed her, when the fact was, she needed you.*

Storme disagreed. Cleo wronged her, entrapped her, and did other despicable things, but she had also been independent, driven, and a giant in business. She learned a lot while being raised by her and kept that separate from the bad stuff.

"Zander gave you the night off for the opening, right? You can stay until the end?"

Phoenix set her on her feet, retrieved her shoe, and knelt before her like her very own Prince Charming. *It wouldn't matter if he didn't. You want me here, I'm here. I'm yours for the whole night.*

"But he did say it's okay, right? I don't want you to get in trouble with your brothers."

Phoenix straightened before her and cupped her jaw in his massive hands. Who would have guessed a man so large and prone to violence could be so incredibly gentle. *Yes, love. They're all coming for the party, and then they'll hit the streets. I'm staying with you, and we'll have a private after-party.*

"We will?" She reached up and clasped her hands around the

back of his neck. "And do I get to know the details of this private shindig after-party?"

He flashed her a lascivious smile and shook his head. *It's a show, don't tell thing. You'll have to wait for the surprise.*

Storme rose to her toes and pulled his mouth down to meet her kiss. He knew how much she loved surprises, and she knew how much he loved her. She couldn't wait. The next week was going to be agony, but with everything Phoenix, he'd make it worth the wait.

His lips were heaven as they moved against hers, warm and hungry, and now so very familiar. How had she ever gotten so lucky? Her mate. Her career. Her future financially and emotionally secure. The only thing that would make it better would be for them to have a baby.

With that thought, she reached between them and accessed the clasp of Phoenix's leathers. The growl that met her lips was all beast, and her body responded immediately.

Shall we christen the lobby, kitten?

Glass windows ran the length of the lobby, but with the lights off, no one would see in. Still, it seemed risqué to go at it right there in the lobby of the hotel. Before she had time to second-guess, his hands were up her dress and tugging down her panties.

"Lights," she gasped, throwing her head back. "Foyer table." After choosing their first target and pulling her dress over her head, she gripped Phoenix's massive shoulders and climbed his body like the jungle cat she was by nature. "Then the registration desk. Then the leather sofas."

She felt his amusement through their magical connection of her being his witch familiar. She was his. She belonged to him. She served him. She resented the implication of what that meant when she first found out, but he never made her feel kept.

They were partners in all things and, if anything, she held the power over him. Their Nephilim mating bond amazed her.

The glass of the six-foot round foyer table was cold on her bare flesh, but she loved the shiver that racked through her.

He pushed his leathers down those tree-trunk, muscled thighs and brought his glistening crown to her heated entrance. Pausing at her pulsing sex, he looked her over.

A goddess lain out for offering.

In *his* mind maybe. Although he did always make her feel like a goddess. "Will you accept the offering, warrior?"

It is my greatest honor in life. Gripping her legs, he pulled her close at the same time he thrust forward. Phoenix's size carried through his entire body, and the invasion of him never ceased to steal her breath. *I love you, kitten.*

She let the purr of her leopard roll from her chest and rejoiced in the moist glide of her mate servicing her. Like all mated Nephilim, they were tireless lovers. She had no doubt that before the night was through, this lobby would be well and truly christened, and she'd be sated to the point of exhaustion.

"I love you too. Now, let's give this hotel something to be proud of. Set the tone for our guests, big man."

Phoenix's laughter made her grateful for every breath she took. This was her life now. He was her life.

As you wish, kitten. May every guest know the love and sexual ecstasy we share here tonight. You know, if it's really transferable, you're going to have a lot of repeat bookings.

～

Danel stepped fully into the parlor and closed his gaping mouth. The scene before him wasn't as alarming as the last one. Why did it seem crazy that Sunshine saw the ghost of Ronnie's dead mother? She saw his angel side, so obviously, she was special. It wasn't common for humans to possess the gift of seeing beyond the veil of the Otherworld, but it happened, usually with children who hadn't learned to be skeptical yet.

"Hello, Scarlett," he said, coming to stand over the two of them playing on the circular carpet. Ronnie's mother was a southern beauty, a natural knockout, like her daughter. Despite her unruly blonde hair, even in death, she exuded the pedigree of the station she once held in life. "It's wonderful to see you again, though I'm sorry it's under these circumstances."

Scarlett rose to greet him, her semi-translucent state common with displaced souls. "The pleasure of having you here is mine, I'm certain. Tell me about Howton. As you can imagine, I've been beside myself since he collapsed."

Danel rubbed a rough hand over his goatee and drew a deep breath. "I'm sorry to be the one to tell you. Your husband suffered a massive stroke. The doctors can do nothing but keep him comfortable until it's over."

She sank onto the arm of the sofa, and raised a hand to her throat. "Is there nothing else to be done? If it's a matter of money, we can fly specialists from anywhere in the world, we can pay for experimental treatments, purchase equipment for the hospital, anything . . ."

He shook his head. "I'm sorry. There's nothing."

She folded her hands in her lap and frowned. "Howton has always been a strong and fierce man. A Titan."

Danel stepped over to the bar cart by the piano and poured a dram of whiskey into a tumbler. "Ronnie's having a hard time coming to terms with it too. Her father is an indestructible force that kept her safe and helped the underdogs of the world. He's her hero."

"Ronnie's daddy's sick," Sunshine said, looking up from the floor with her stuffed gray kitty. "He's in a big bed at the hosbidal."

Danel set the tumbler down untouched and joined his girl on the rug. "Yes, he is. The angels will come for him soon."

"Then he be with my mommy?"

Danel nodded. "That's right."

"That's nice," she said, tilting her head to the side. "They can be friends."

"I'm sure they will be the best of friends." The gray ball of fur in her lap moved, and he smiled. "My goodness. Who is this? Did Kitty come to life?"

"No, silly," she said, laughing as she bopped the kitten's head and made it blink. "This is Rascal. He's a baby, so we gotsta be gentle."

He pointed to the fine scratches marking the flesh on her arm. "It doesn't look like Rascal was gentle with you. Do those hurt, sweet girl?"

"I made hims mad." She poked the thin lines across her arm and frowned. "I don't do that no more. I's gentle, right Ronnie's mama?"

Scarlett lowered herself to join them on the plush rug. "That's right. If you're rough with him, he's rough with you."

"That's how a lot of things work, monkey," Danel said, stroking the kitten's ear. "You get back what you put out in the world, so it's best to put out love and happiness, right?"

"And sunshine. Like my song."

He winked. "Exactly. Now, enough with the kitten. Let's go clean those scratches and find you a bandage, shall we?"

He scooped her into his arms, but stopped when her face fell and her eyes started to well up. "Why the sad face?"

"Rascal's sorry. He's lonely and wantsa play."

Danel rolled his eyes and scooped the gray furball up too. "He can come, but no more scratches. It's my job to make sure no one hurts you, right?"

Sunshine squished the kitten to her chest and nodded. "He be good. Promise."

He chuckled and kissed her cheek. When he got to the door, he turned back to Scarlett. The woman was the spitting image of Ronnie, and it broke his heart to see her looking so solemn. "We're heading back to the hospital first thing in the morning. I'll keep you posted. And again, Scarlett, I'm so sorry for your loss."

CHAPTER SEVEN

A flash of pain jolted Colt awake and something struck him with a loud *bang*. His head hurt, his mouth tasted dry and bad—like he'd eaten roadkill and then not brushed his teeth for a week—and there was an excruciating pain in his right shoulder that made him wonder if he'd been hit by a rocket launcher.

Still dark out. Stank of rotting garbage.

He lifted his head and wiped his mouth with the back of his hand. As his thoughts crept toward the edges of clarity, he realized he remained ass-planted in the side-alley across from Storme's hotel. The only difference between now and when he'd passed out, was now, he wasn't alone.

He felt, more than saw, what faced him.

Well, "face" was a stretch because the body of the creature wasn't solid. Its features shifted in heaving waves as it breathed. Was *breathed* the right word? Hard to know. Standing fifteen feet away, in what he interpreted as a hostile stance, its limbs and core undulated and buzzed—entirely made of flies.

Um, okay, this wasn't good.

"Who summoned you, demon?" he demanded, his voice rasping like he'd swallowed barbed wire.

The creature swung forward, the swarm of flies gathering in a great gauntlet that shot toward him like something out of Saturday cartoons. The blow struck him square in the chest.

The impact stole his breath and broke more than one rib. Runnels of magic dripped warmly down his chest and dug into his organs like an invasion of hot metal.

Gasping, he tried not to pass out.

Soooo not an ordinary daemon.

Colt racked his brain, searching through the tomes of lore he'd studied as a boy. Shit. Yep. He was pooched. "Asmodeus, Prince of Demons, what have I done to offend you?"

The swarm of flies that struck him rejoined the collective of the daemon's form and the beast swelled in size. "You consort with Nephilim assassins and fornicate with the Celtic General."

Uh-huh. The Hell Realm rumor-mill was fast, but not that fast. *Fucking Andz'gar.* If Colt had put any stock into his family connection with his cousin, he might've been disappointed. As it was, he was impressed with his decisiveness—as well as thoroughly annoyed.

"The Ice Demon King summoned you. Why? To kill me? To teach me a lesson?" He gave his cousin props. He didn't think the asshole had enough weight in his nutsack to draw such a line in the sand.

"The man-whore must not ascend."

Ascend? The word struck him cold.

Being marked by Andz'gar for sexing it up with Brennus was bad. This was worse—much worse.

For Asmodeus to declare ascension in his mission, it meant that Andz'gar knew the Pandora's box of their ancestry had opened. He wasn't smart enough to put that together. Someone from his Hell Realm rehab team sold him out.

Fucking Darkworlders—you couldn't trust them.

He hadn't meant for it to happen.

He'd lost himself, true, but the moment he felt the kernel of icy power grow within, he'd slammed the box shut, bolted the lid closed, and duct-taped the shit outta the thing.

What more did Andz'gar want?

"Your king wants you dead."

Aww, perfect. Thanks for clearing that up. "The only problem with that is . . . *I* don't want to be dead. Nor do I want to ascend. Tell the Ice King there's no issue. He can keep on keepin' on, and we don't ever have to see one another again."

"The man-whore must not ascend."

Okay, repeating that didn't make anything better.

Colt rolled to his knees and pushed himself to a crouch. Given two massive hits from a greater demon, he wasn't sure he could trust his legs. The closer to the ground he remained, the shorter the distance to fall.

He was better off biding his time to gather energy.

There were broken bits inside him, his breathing labored and wheezy. His chest hurt like a mofo, and the shaky, light-headed effects of his self-pity drinking-binge had worn off.

This wasn't his night.

Without drawing attention to his movements, he eased off his leather gloves and exposed the only weapons he'd have against a Prince of Demons if this came to a fight.

Shit. He hoped that wasn't the way this went.

～

Storme giggled at the size of her husband's ego as he escorted her out the back door hours after they'd gotten naked. Basking in his achievements, this was a true "cock-o-the-walk" moment for him. The sexual christening of the foyer was amazing, but sex with Phoenix was always amazing. The male had talents she didn't like to think about because you don't get to that level of proficiency with a woman's body without an incredible amount of practice.

Nope. Not going there. Ever.

And it wasn't the sex that had him strutting his stuff. What cranked up the Egyptian smug-o-meter was somehow, he swore he could sense they made a baby.

How he knew mystified her, but after his transition to a Dark Angel and absorbing his evil mother's magic, his powers defied all explanation. Even though Storme wasn't ready to go out and buy a stroller and a car seat yet—she hoped he was right. Man, did she ever hope he was right.

What do you think of calling her Arya?

She stopped to set the alarm system and lock the door. "We are *not* naming our child based on a fictional character from *The Game of Thrones*."

A strong, kick-ass character, who took no shit.

"Our child, if there is one, will inherit enough kick-assery from her parents and her uncles. And what makes you think it's a she? There is *noooo* way you can tell that."

No, but I want a little girl. I want her to look just like you, and smile like you, and see the world as a great adventure to conquer, just like her mom.

Mom. She loved the sound of that.

She held out her keys and beeped off the alarm on her car. A wave of Darkworld energy slammed into them, and Phoenix caught her elbow when she staggered. It was an eerie pervasive feeling, a repugnant invasion of heebie-jeebies crawling under her skin. "What is that?"

They both turned toward the street but saw nothing.

Phoenix's cocky smile morphed into a look of deadly warning. His Mark lit up, and he pointed to her vehicle alone in the lot. *Get in and lock the doors. Straight home, kitten.*

"What? No. I'm your partner . . ." Finishing the sentence was moot because he'd launched into the darkness of the night sky and was gone.

Despite being annoyed at the dismissal, she sank into the driver's seat and locked the doors as he instructed. Bonded Nephilim needed their females to be safe, the wives understood that, but out-of-control dark witches needed their familiars to level out their powers.

Which was she in this situation—mate or familiar?

Deciding that women of today could be more than one thing, she started the car and drove to the front of the property. Stopping before the road, she slid the shifter into park, leaned forward, and stared out the front and side windows.

Where did he go? What had they felt?

Closing her eyes, she reached out for Phoenix following the magical bond that tied them. Envisioning the gossamer strands attached to the velvet choker she wore, she saw it stretch into the darkness like the shimmering silk of a spider.

That was their Master/familiar bond.

It had no weight, and its tensile strength was unbreakable.

She plucked the strands with the lightest of touches, a slight pat on a magical violin string. The vibration shimmered in the light of the moon overhead, and she followed it with her gaze. She kept the signal weak, hoping Phoenix didn't feel her inquiry from his end.

The last thing she wanted was to distract him if he was busy fighting evil. If she admitted the truth, she also didn't want to cross his wishes if no issue existed.

She needn't have worried.

As if her attention summoned the opening of the gates of Hell, an explosion of magic lit the side-alley cattycorner from the hotel. Turning off the car, she got out and raised her hands.

She knew three spells of concealment off the top of her head, and she began the incantation to cast the most powerful.

Palms forward, she cloaked first herself, and then stretched the shield toward what was quite literally, all Hell breaking loose.

Fights happened very fast. That was even truer when those fighting were members of the Otherworld. She'd heard about a few that lasted longer because of the strength of the combatants or the sheer number of daemons involved, but even then, time rushed by in seconds and minutes—not longer.

That simply meant that she needed to act fast and hold on tight until the ride came to a full and complete stop. The conflict erupted, in gunshots, a furious wailing noise, and a lightning storm of gold and green. The stench of hellfire and brimstone choked the night air. Strengthening her commands, she spread her stance and focused.

A battle here seemed awfully . . . in the middle of things.

The one tenet members of the Otherworld lived by, and agreed on, was "Don't spook the townsfolk." Whatever the event erupting before her, it would've been better in an area less densely populated, with a few less thousand prying eyes to bear witness.

Thus, the concealment spell.

She'd been part of the magic world her whole life. It ran in her blood as a Shadow Caster shifter, it had been taught to her by her mentor, Cleo Queen, and it surrounded her day and night, pulsing as a living entity from her husband.

This, more than business owner, was her wheelhouse.

Focused as she was on containing the impact of the light show in front of her, she missed the inundation of vermin. The panicked squeaking of a thousand rats brought her attention to the writhing brown, furry bodies brushing her ankles and stampeding over her feet.

Either Phoenix battled the Pied Piper or the rodents of the city had banded together to take Toronto.

Cursing, she scuffed her Jimmy Choos across the concrete

sidewalk, shuffling backward against the rushing flow of vermin bodies. Retreating into the car wasn't easy while still casting the enchantment, but she managed.

She was doing her part for the cause.

She hoped Phoenix could take care of the rest.

Who says married life gets boring?

~

Phoenix opened his wings and launched above the onslaught of a thousand rats moving as one. Fuckety-fuck-fuck. He hovered for a moment, staring at the now vacant alley before turning back. He'd failed Colt. Wherever that buzzing bastard took the cop, he wasn't in good shape. Reeling from the fight and losing a friend to a greater power, he closed the distance between him and the white Mercedes that should not have been idling fifty yards away.

I told you to go home.

Storme rolled the window down. "I stayed out of the line of fire and concealed the battle from prying eyes. Stop glaring at me and tell me what happened."

What happened? You put yourself in harm's way. There was a greater demon loose on the streets, and you disobeyed me and put yourself in its path.

He scrubbed rough fingers over his skull-trim and cursed. Wound as he was, with his beast driving the train, he was about to say or do something he'd regret.

Go home. Straight home.

He launched into the night as far and as fast as his strength and magic shot him. Wind slapped his face and burned his eyes, but he didn't feel the discomfort. He was numb, and at the same time, hypersensitive to everything around him.

When he stopped ascending and fell back toward the city, he

let his mass freefall. Adrenaline raced through his veins, and he plummeted toward the lights of the city. Before he fell low enough to become visible to humans, he opened his wings and found her car.

He followed Storme home, waited until the taillights of her car disappeared down the slope of the underground parking garage, then flew to the front steps of the ranch house and entered the vestibule. Sticking his face in front of the security scanner, he let the retinal recognition do its thing.

As he strode toward the war room, he met Tanek exiting the kitchen. Raising his hands, he realized he was covered in blood. *Call everyone in. We've got a serious problem.*

∼

Brennus raced down the main corridor of the ranch, his beast raging, his heart pumping like a firehose. Tanek's message was, *Get back ASAP. Colt taken.* Taken? His beast was weighing in heavy on that, and the warrior wasn't a fan either. His shit-kickers squeaked on the polished floor as he banked right into the war room. The gang was all there, minus Danel, of course. Phoenix was a bloody mess, Zander looked murderous, and the rest of his brothers were drinking and fidgeting like live wires.

"What do we know fer sure?"

His brothers looked over at him, and their eyes widened.

"Where the hell were you?" Zander asked.

"Nice knees, Celt," Seth said, pointing to the bottom hem of his kilt. "Consider shaving your legs next time. Manscaping is a thing these days."

Fuck. He forgot he still wore his dress clothes from dinner with Jack. Damn, guilt stabbed him in the gut that he'd been out on the town having a lovely evening while Colton had been the victim of some heinous attack.

"Forget my kilt and focus," he snapped. His beast seethed too close to the surface for his voice not to sound strangled. "And while yer at it, tell me what the fuck happened."

While Zander relayed Phoenix's account of the night's battle against a greater demon, Brennus stormed over to the bar, poured himself a healthy dose of Zander's high-end scotch, and hammered it back.

"Any idea who took him?"

"My guess is Asmodeus," Danel said, out of a speaker somewhere by the desk. Zander nodded to the screen of his computer, so he figured the Persian had Skyped in. "Of the seven Princes of Demons, he's one of the more well-known, because he's one of the easiest to summon and put to task."

"What task?" Brennus asked. "And summoned by who?"

He kept repeating, the man-whore must not ascend.

"Man-whore is judgy," Seth said, scowling. "Sexing it up on the regular isn't a crime, or Phoenix and I would've been dragged away centuries ago."

"Ascend to what?" Hark asked. "Ice Demons already have a king, and the cop isn't exactly driven by ambition."

"Forget *why* he took him," Brennus snapped. "*Where* did he take him, and how do we get him back?"

Zander looked at his computer screen. "Do you have any ideas on the where, D?"

"Not really. It depends who summoned him, and what the contract stipulated was to be done with him."

"Can we track him?" Bo asked. "Can Storme or Phoenix cast a spell and scry his location?"

Zander looked to Phoenix on that one. The guy didn't look like his beast would let Storme out of his sight for oh . . . maybe a century. *Storme's better with spells than I am. She's the finesse. I'm brute power. Even if we worked together, I doubt we could amp the signal enough to reach the shadows of the Hell Realm.*

"What about a blood spell?" Seth asked. "Those hold a lot more oomph."

Phoenix shrugged. *Have you got Colt's blood handy?*

Zander sighed. "Okay, keep your thinking caps on. First things first. What's our risk of exposure?"

Nada. Storme dropped a veil around the fight and kept things private. No exposure, except maybe people freaking out about the fly and rat infestation. Nothing Otherworld though.

"Storme dropped the veil?" Bo said, leaning forward in his seat on the leather sofa.

Phoenix's Mark burst into a vibrant shade of neon green.

"Why was your female on the streets?" the Viking asked.

She wasn't. I went to escort her home. This happened right across the street from her hotel. Colt had hunkered down in the alley for some reason. His bike was there, and he'd knocked off quite an impressive selection from the liquor store.

Zander shook his head, his long hair loose and swaying with the movement. "None of this adds up. Why would the cop come back after being missing for almost two months and camp out to get drunk in an alley across from Storme's hotel?"

The man-whore must not ascend.

"Fuck me," Brennus hissed, his heart cleaving in two. This was his fault. This was about him. He didn't know how he knew it so definitively, but he did.

Stay the fuck away from me, Celt.

More pouring, more drinking. He finished the second and then the third shot. When he turned around, the room spun, but not enough to miss that his brothers were staring.

"Something on your mind, Celt?" Zander asked.

Brennus scrubbed his palms over his face. His cheeks were numb, and he wished he could go somewhere and finish the job. "Before I say anything, let me remind each and every one of ye that self-destructive, bad decisions run in our blood. Ye all agree with that, aye?"

It wasn't anything they could deny.

"Fair enough," Zander said. "We're all violent meatheads that act as our own worst enemies most of the time."

Everyone agreed with that.

Brennus tried to think what he could say that might get them to where they needed to be without waving his private business in the air for all to see.

"Brennus? For fuck's sake, spit it out."

There was no way around it. This was gonna suck.

Drawing a deep breath, he let the words fly. "Ye see, the cop and I, we've been fucking around, and it got away on us."

Cue the chorus of sharp inhales around the room.

"Since *when*?" Zander shouted, grinding his fists into the top of his desk. "He's our biggest asset, Brennus. What the fuck were you thinking?"

"Ye say that like either of us was thinkin'."

Zander scowled. "How long?"

"Off and on since the day Seth lay dying in the clinic. Things looked bad, and there was a lot of emotion in the air."

"That was almost five months ago. Why the hell didn't you mention this before now?"

Brennus shrugged. "It wasna a regular thing. Just an outlet when shite got intense."

Zander cocked his head like he didn't believe that. "Shit's been intense for months. So, what? You think the man-whore reference is your fault?"

Brennus nodded, though he refused to think of what he and Colt got up to as being wrong. Two consenting adults. Behind closed doors. Well, he couldn't claim that one, they'd never once been somewhere private. But that was another story.

"He called it off the night he disappeared."

"The night the council meeting got highjacked."

He nodded. "Aye, I couldna get up to the loft to help ye, and my beast and I were both wild. Cop saw me flirtin' with Jack, and that set him off. Things got outta hand—even for us. It was bad. I thought I mighta killed him."

Zander rounded the corner of his desk and sat on the edge. There was a softening of his fury that Brennus wasn't prepared for. He was baring ugly secrets, and his commander looked at him with compassion.

He didn't want that. He didn't deserve it.

"That was the night Colt fell off the face of the planet. You think that was because of you?"

It made him sick to think of it now. He should have fought harder. He should have been stronger. "Aye, I was sure of it."

"Why, B?"

He dropped his head back and stared at the tin ceiling tiles. "He fed from me."

"He *what*?" Zander's voice rang out, and lightning struck outside. Gone was the understanding brother. In his place was the violent, brutal Sumerian.

Zander rose to his full height and got face-to-face, his wings up and spread. When he spoke next, his voice was eerily quiet and tight. "Colt Creed is our strongest ally in this war, and you could've killed him. He went dark for weeks, missing without a trace. He could've died. His system could've taken what we are and changed him—"

"Don't ye think I *know* that?" Brennus stepped back, his heartbeat pounding so hard he could barely think. "Don't ye think I searched for him, imagining all the horrible possibilities. He's your friend, Z, and you're out of yer mind. I was his lover. I'm the one who put him in that situation. What do ye think that did to *me*?"

Zander's eyes widened sharply, lingering on Brennus's Mark as the tattooed fretwork covering his body flared a brilliant silver. Shite.

This *Dear Abby* bullshit wasn't doing his control over his beast any good. It wasn't bonding, because he and Colt weren't anywhere near a happily-ever-after, so it must be a case of his beast exerting his frustration.

"Okaaaay," Tanek said after a long silence. "So, with the relationship stuff on the table, we have more insight. Phoenix, how about you speak to Storme about the scrying idea. Obvi, we have a blood source now, if Colt's out there and he fed from Brennus. Danel, keep digging on Asmodeus. Seth and Hark, you're on the cousin. If there's one person that won't want Colt to ascend to something, it'll be the man currently in power. Bo, go back to the alley and clean up the mess."

With tasks assigned, the room cleared, and that left him and Zander staring each other down. "I'm pissed ten different ways about this, Celt," Zander said, shaking his head. "It never should've happened, and when it did, you should have ended it. When you didn't, you should've told me, and when he disappeared, you should've told me again."

Zander closed his eyes and pinched the bridge of his nose, a habit he'd developed when the pressures of being garrison commander overwhelmed.

Brennus drew a deep breath and stepped back, pleased to see his Mark had run out of batteries and returned to normal. "I fucked up, Z. I ken that better than anyone, but it wasna because either of us was careless or didna recognize the seriousness of our situation. Colt and I were explosive together. Like gasoline and flame."

"Were?"

Brennus headed back over to the bar and poured two drinks. Coming back to his commander, he held out the peace offering. "Colt broke it off when he left, and again two nights ago when he got back. It felt all wrong, but I didna press his decision. We both knew it was doomed."

"Do you believe that?"

Brennus sipped at his tumbler and nodded. "I did. At least, I tried to. I think Colt was camped out tonight because I had a date with Jack. I picked the lad up at the hotel earlier, and I felt like someone was watching us. In hindsight, I'm sure it was him. Something's not right, Z. I'd bet my life him cutting ties isna as simple as he pretended."

Zander sighed and sucked back his scotch. "With affairs of the heart, my brother, it never is."

CHAPTER EIGHT

The first thing Colt thought, as he rose from the depths of unconsciousness, was that he hated being dead. It sucked. He never gave into the whole afterlife, better place, bullshit. After all—helloooo, child of Hell here. Still, he'd hoped, at the very least, it wouldn't be so hot. Yeah, yeah, Hell was hot, he got that, but why did the afterlife have to be hot?

And what was with the noise?

There was a *pat-pat-pat* sound somewhere on his right, and the wheeze of a leaking balloon somewhere on his left. He tried to draw breath and got a stabbing reminder of broken ribs.

Asmodeous's super-fly jab did a serious number on him. Shouldn't the pain and suffering be over, now that he was dead? As a sadist, maybe this was his afterlife, and it was supposed to work for him?

It wasn't.

He cracked an eyelid and realized the *pat-pat-pat* sound was his blood dripping from the tips of his toes onto the plasma-blackened dirt floor, and the whistling tune of leaking balloon was air escaping his punctured lung.

Nice, he'd always wanted to be a musician.

He wondered how Phoenix faired. That warrior was a military tank before he mated, and then with the dark powers, and transitioning to a full Dark Angel, yeah, now he was one scary powerful beast. Colt was sure the guy would've gotten away clean once Asmodeus snagged him for take-home.

He closed his eyes, and tried to draw breath in tiny bursts. Didn't help. The only silver lining to his slow suffocation was that it pretty much proved he wasn't dead. Or maybe he was and was stuck in a *Groundhog Day* nightmare loop that would keep him reliving this torture over and over again.

That idea had merit.

Didn't matter. If he wasn't dead yet, he'd get there soon enough. There was no reason Asmodeus would keep him alive. *The man-whore must not ascend,* right?

Fuck you, Andz'gar.

He tried again to fill his lungs and decided he preferred suffocation over the pain of what felt like Z's new Hummer driving over his chest. It pissed him off that he was going to die before he even got a ride in that blue beast.

How long had he been here? How long would Asmodeus let him live? The seven Princes of Demons weren't known for their warm and fuzzies. They were lethal, delivering swift and brutal sentences.

So, if he was supposed to be dead, why wasn't he?

The man-whore must not ascend.

The answer struck him like the blackout curtains opening and the summer sun shining in. Laughter bubbled up from his chest, and he cut that shit out before he blacked out.

Masters had to be very specific when summoning a demon and setting it to right a wrong. Greater demons were cunning bastards. No subtext. No insinuation. No interpretations.

Dimes to dog-nuts, Andz'gar didn't get it right.

His cousin charged Asmodeus with not allowing him to ascend. He hadn't told the Prince of Demons to kill him, at least not directly, or that's what he would have done. He might be a prisoner forever, but for now, he'd take it and not complain.

He exhaled and sank into his bindings. The stretch of his arms over his head made it excruciating to breathe, but for that moment, he didn't care.

Thank the Dark Prince his cousin was an idiot.

Feeling like he'd won the fuck-you lottery, he looked around his digs: standard torture scene—a dank, vacuous cave with a dirt floor and rough stone walls. His wrists were bound and strung from a steel hoop high above his head. It dangled him like a pheasant waiting to be cooked up for dinner.

The stench of death, rot, and every sort of bodily fluid and excrement filled the air to the point of his eyes watering.

Well, this was hell after all.

"You wake."

He turned toward the mouth of the cave and eyed the female staring at him. Far from lovely, her face was broad and heavily scarred, her eyes small and coal black, and her mouth held rows of spiny teeth that spilled out and touched her top lip like a lap dog with an underbite. What hair she had was pulled up and back on one side, like an '80s throwback. He had no creds being a fashion critic, but even he knew it was an unfortunate choice.

"Yes, I'm awake."

"Brar'don, cousin of the Ice King, member of the Royal House of Stregious," she said, her voice weighted as if she were announcing him to a grand ballroom full of attendees, "you are now a guest of the seven Princes of Demons."

"I'd bow, but my feet don't touch the floor."

The woman paid him no attention. She grabbed a skeletal broom and started swiping at the littered dirt floor. He looked at the bones and the rot and the piles of shit, and wondered if she thought a little sweeping would do the trick.

"So, what does it mean to be a guest of the seven Princes? Do

I get an invite to the parties? Will there be a dinner in my honor? Will I *be* the dinner at my party?"

The female whacked him in the side with her wooden broomstick, and he cursed her a thousand deaths. "You think you're funny. You are not. You sexed with filthy Watchers. It disgusts and shames us all. Shame. Shame. Shame."

Technically, he sexed with *one* Watcher, but clarifying that wouldn't likely gain him points. More importantly, she was wrong. He was damn funny. And she sounded like the zealots on *The Game of Thrones.* Shame. Shame. Shame.

Fuck shame. He didn't play that game.

The handful of encounters he'd had with the Celt were hands down the most memorable moments of his pathetic love life. He wasn't saying that his experiences were pathetic. He had enjoyed decades of hedonistic orgies and gatherings, men, women, males, females—he didn't discriminate.

If they got caught in his dicksand, he'd do them.

The only things that mattered were a level of attraction, full consent, avoiding nasty aftereffects, and everyone walking away with a smile on their face.

He didn't see a problem with that.

Then again, he didn't weigh things with the same scale as others did. Daemons had a bad habit of pointing fingers and dictating to anyone who would listen what others were doing wrong. Judgment. Rumors. Caustic backstabbing.

It was one of the main reasons he left the Hell Realm in the first place. It was also one of the reasons he enjoyed his trysts with Brennus. The male led much the same life with the same values. He didn't judge. He didn't get possessive.

Hell, Colt had dropped him like a hot rock, and the guy had barely blinked. Okay, that wasn't great.

He would've liked the General to be upset, maybe lose a few pounds pining away for him for a year or two.

At least six months.

Instead, he'd made a date with that Ken doll the next night.

"Where's Asmodeus?" he said, pushing that reality to the *waaaay* back of his mind. "His guest would like a word."

"He's gone."

"Gone where? When will he be back?"

"Can't say. He's *my* Master, not the other way."

Colt tried for what he hoped was a sexy smile. "You know, if he's not around, there's no reason for me to hang up here. I'd love to take a piss. You have no idea how much alcohol I took in earlier. There's a limit to what a bladder can hold."

"You're naked. Piss all over yourself. I don't care."

"You're a terrible hostess. I'm just sayin'."

Another whack with the broom handle had him gasping rancid air but taking none into his lungs. The wheeze ramped up from a leaky balloon to a dying dog.

Motherfucker, that hurt.

～

Phoenix took the stairs two at a time up to the suite at the end of the third floor. Damn. How had their night gone from one extreme to the other end of the scale? He wanted the joy of their sex play back. He wanted—

The scent of Storme's tears tainted the air outside their suite. He broke into a run, his beast roaring in his ears. He found his mate on one of the leather couches, Thea holding her hand, consoling her. Physically, she was perfect. She didn't seem injured, and there was no trace of blood. That meant—the two of them looked up—yep, this was all his doing.

Thea rose as he entered the room and whatever she saw in his face had her pulling a hasty retreat for the bedroom she shared with his brother. "Sleep well," she said. "Both of you."

When the latch of the bedroom door clicked shut, he rounded the couch and dropped to his knee. Storme's eyes were

86

swollen and red-rimmed, her makeup staining her cheeks. He reached to take the hand Thea held, but it was withdrawn.

The denial to touch her, to comfort her, was more than his beast could take. Whatever he had done, he'd undo. Whatever he'd damaged, he would fix. The only thing that mattered to him in life was that his mate thrive.

He needed her happy and healthy.

I understand this is my fault, he said through their mental connection. *In a moment of anger and frustration, I found you in the path of danger and my most primal instincts of protection reared. I was short with you, and I apologize, from the depth of my soul.*

She glared at him and shook her head. "You were short with me? You think that's what this is about?"

Okaaaay, so maybe not. He pumped more power to his cranium, and got his hamster running. They'd been rock-solid, then the fight with Asmodeus, then he'd snapped at her, now he was in deep dog-house territory.

I admit. I don't understand.

She frowned, disappointment heavy in her stormy gaze. "Think harder."

He went back again but still didn't see. *We had an amazing session in the foyer. We were good then.*

She nodded but didn't give him more than that.

Then I got my ass kicked by a greater demon and Colt was taken prisoner because I failed him.

Her mouth gaped, and the scent of concern took away some of the pain and betrayal. Still, she didn't let him off the hook, so he kept on it.

Then I sensed your magic, and realized you were in the thick of things. My pride and anger stung from losing Colt, and I didn't want my fear for you to lash out. I told you to come home. I kept my distance so I didn't say something I couldn't take back. I followed you from above, and once the garage door sealed, I went to report Colt's abduction to the garrison.

She shook her head, and a fresh round of tears fell.

Shit. His Mark exploded green as his beast reeled. He was making this worse. His fear of losing her tonight hit him with a powerful second wave, and tears stung his eyes as well.

Help me understand, kitten? I'm fucking something up here, and I don't know what. Let me fix it, please. I can face anything except you shutting me out and being angry.

She locked eyes with him. "Bingo. You're there."

He was? He backtracked. *I did that to you. I was angry and shut you out.*

"And left me in the cold for hours. I didn't know about Colt, or what happened in the fight, or that you even cared enough to follow me. You just ordered me home and left."

His vision of her blurred at the same time his cheeks heated with runnels of tears. W.T.F. She didn't know he cared enough to follow her home? That cleaved his heart, a dagger ripping his life-beating organ into two shredded halves.

By all that's good and right in this world, I didn't realize I did that. I apologize. But how can you say you're surprised I followed you home? Don't you understand who you are to me? Haven't I shown you —proven *to you every night and day—that you are the only thing in the three realms I need to survive?*

"You were *so* angry."

His entire body shook, his beast raging, his world's foundation rumbling beneath his feet. *At the thought of you getting hurt. At my failure in that fight. In my worry that Colt will die because I wasn't good enough or strong enough or smart enough to save him.*

"I didn't know any of that! You didn't tell me and you didn't come to tell me until now."

He swiped his eyes with rough hands and put a stop to the waterworks. He was a warrior. He knew where he'd erred, and he needed fix this before he lost his mind. *I love you, Storme. Nothing will ever change that. Not anger. Not fear. Not your defiance. You are my soul. I know you wives think you understand what that means to us, but you don't. You can't. Take what you imagine my devotion to be and multiply it a thousand times. Then make it unbreakable, and then make it feed every atom in every cell of my being. Then still, that doesn't cover it.* You are everything to me, *kitten.* Everything.

His hands trembled as he reached for her touch. *Please, I beg you, let me hold you. I'm losing my grip here.*

She seemed to take stock of his hold on his powers, and realized they were in dark magic meltdown territory. She gripped his wrists and pulled him forward.

He folded into her lap and wrapped his arms around her back. She rubbed circles on his back, settling the volatility in his powers, easing his turmoil so he could regain control.

If I fuck up, just tell me, please. Don't pull away from me. I'm not strong enough to take it.

⁓

Storme squeezed her eyes closed, fighting to ease the magical instability she'd caused in her husband. Not strong enough? The powers that he possessed terrified her. How he had the strength to carry the burden astounded her. She needed to be more aware of the dangers and not add to them.

"I thought you were punishing me for disobeying you. I drove out to the street, and the battle exploded. I knew you wanted me to leave, but my first instinct was to help you. I may not be a warrior, but concealment was something I could do."

Phoenix pulled back and looked up at her. His eyes were glassy, and she hated she'd hurt him so deeply.

I would never leave you alone to fight. I understand it is no different for you. I may want you clear of the dangers of my life, but you're a survivor, Storme. I recognize how talented you are. I feel how powerful. If you are in trouble, I know you can draw my power to keep you from harm. Still, I worry.

89

"Okay," she said, blinking back another crying jag and fanning her eyes, "that was a really good answer."

He sat on the couch and pulled her into his lap. *It's true, I swear. I look at you, and beyond the devastating beauty, I see my partner—an equal. You inspire me day and night. I'm sorry you don't know that without being told. I guess I'm not as good at this relationship stuff as I thought. I'm sorry about that too.*

Shaking her head, she tucked her face against his neck. Nuzzling the wide choker that both covered his scar and marked him as the Master of their magical pairing, she sighed. "We're going to have moments, every couple does. Please don't shut me out again."

On my honor, I do so swear.

She liked it when he talked that ancient warrior talk. "Say that again in your language?"

Which one, Egyptian or Enochian?

"Both."

He repeated his pledge to her twice more, and she felt their world right itself once more. "Take me to bed, sexy man. I hear make-up sex is the best."

His chest bounced under her ears, and he stroked her arm. *That has to wait, I'm afraid. We need your help with a blood scrying spell strong enough to reach the Hell Realm. Then, hopefully, I'll be going to bring Colt home.*

Wow. That was one heck of a range.

She didn't even know where to start. She hugged Phoenix and nodded. They'd figure it out. "All right. Raincheck on the make-up sex."

CHAPTER NINE

*D*anel looked up from his laptop and rose from Ronnie's high school desk. His blurry vision sharpened in an instant, his entire body attuned to his mate. Rest hadn't touched the sadness in her eyes, but fresh from their bed, she seemed sturdier on her feet than she had been the day before.

"Hey, beautiful. I hope I didn't wake you."

She smiled, accepting the invitation of his open arms, and came in for full-bodied contact. Wrapping herself around his thick waist, she leaned into him and linked her fingers against his bare back. "After last night, I slept like the dead."

He winced at her words, hating that reference even if it was a human figure of speech. Her kind was too fragile—her father lying in a hospital bed, dying, case in point. He and his beast within couldn't handle the thought of Ronnie not being with him for eternity.

He believed she would be. If his semen healed her from her human disease, in theory, it should also halt her aging and dying process. The other brothers wondered if that theory would transfer to their mates too.

There were still so many unknowns in Nephilim mating.

She tilted her face up to him, brushing his cheek. "You were up early. Is everything all right?"

He kissed her, a gentle touch of their mouths, and filled his lungs to their depths with her scent. The glorious perfume mixed the aromas of her shampoo, the residue from their hours of lovemaking, and her concern for him.

Who needed sleep when his entire existence, the very reason he suffered through millennia of violence and abuse, was to be the man he was today for this female?

"I'm fine, luv. Even better now that you're in my arms."

In truth, he hadn't slept at all. He had been lying in their bed, holding her naked body after chasing her fears away as she'd asked, when Tanek called everyone in. He'd Skyped into the meeting and then searched ancient texts all night.

His resources here were severely limited. At home, he had scrolls and chronicles and tomes of reference. None of them were digitized, and that left him with his hands tied. When he got home, he would put Ringo on that.

They'd work together to ensure this didn't happen again.

"Kang is meeting me at the hospital this morning. His scribe agreed to loan me some texts, since my reference library isn't accessible right now."

"Do you need to go back?" Her gaze sharpened and he could see her gauging his response. She'd send him packing if she thought he was needed elsewhere—if she knew Colt's life hung in the balance—but his life depended on him being here for her.

"No. It's a research project for Zander. I'm fine working with the local garrison."

Ronnie's head canted to the side like she was deciding whether or not to buy what he was selling. "Maybe you should go to Kang's clubhouse for a few hours. That makes more sense than him bringing a library to you. If Kang's scribe is anything like you, a semi-truck couldn't move all the books."

He flashed her a grin. "I do have an impressive collection, don't I?" He chuckled and shook his head. "No matter. The search is specific and shouldn't involve more than three or four books, half a dozen at the most. I'll deal. And I'll do it next to you, in case you need me."

Ronnie blinked up at him, her gaze soft, her smile coy. "I always need you. In fact, I think I need your help in the shower to wash my back."

Danel scooped Ronnie into his arms and headed to her suite's private bath. "How long until Sunshine wakes up?"

"An hour?"

Danel nodded. "All right, get ready for the best fifty-seven-minute shower you've ever had."

"Fifty-seven?"

He nodded. "We have to leave a buffer to get dried and dressed. Geez, woman, you're insatiable."

Ronnie's laughter fed his soul. It truly did.

~

Brennus roused from his nap on one of the four couches in the war room. He fought the return to the real world, caught up in a dream that had him fighting back-to-back with Colt, whipping a double-pointed spear through the air, cutting down a thousand daemons who rushed in at them as a horde and smelled like French toast. The battle he understood, the male too, but what was the French toast part about?

"Good, you're awake," Seth said, giving his shoulder a shake. "Come see where we are. Storme verified that Colt is still alive, but we need more blood to pin down where."

Thank fuck. Still alive was what he wanted to hear. Wait. How long had he slept? He hadn't heard Seth come in. Had he been that out of it?

A man could only run on hope and adrenaline for so many

hours before the crash hit. In his mind's eye, he pictured Storme drawing a blade across his palm, dripping his essence into a mixing bowl with herbs and eyes and webs from rare spiders, and *poof*, her wee pendulum would point them in a direction.

Real life wasn't a TV show.

She and Phoenix had poured over mixtures, discussing the properties of ingredients, and took a really-fucking-*loooong* time coming up with a plan. Not that he'd complain.

Not dead was amazing news and now he was rested up for the next phase of this plan.

Rescuing his estranged lover.

He rubbed his palms over his face and shook himself awake. The scene looked the same as it had—he checked his watch— over four hours ago.

Wow, he *had* crashed.

Getting to his feet, he stretched. His shoulder popped and his muscles let loose from their stiffness. He twisted and saw the breakfast feast heaped in the corner.

Ah, that explained the French toast.

"More blood ye say, weel yer in luck. One willing plasma juice box at yer service. Stick me. Stab me. Whatever ye need."

He met Storme, dagger in hand, and let her do her thing. "We'll get you there, Red. I have a good feeling."

Phoenix nodded and raised his hands. *What we need now is for Danel to tell us what to do when we get there. I fought this fucker. We'll only get one shot at this.*

~

Ronnie sat at the side of her father's hospital bed, telling him anything she hadn't mentioned during their scheduled Sunday night catch-up call over the past months. The thought that they'd never do that again stole her breath. She hated to think he was suffering, but the doctors assured her he wasn't.

"The scratches weren't bad, but Danel was annoyed that anything would dare harm his precious girl." She knew he, of all people, would understand that instinct, because he'd been as aggressively protective of her growing up.

"Sunshine didn't let him get away with him exiling her kitty, though. Oh no, Rascal was a gift from Aibileen and there was no undoing that. She's got him wrapped around her little finger. I wish you could've met her properly . . ."

She almost said, "before you die," but wasn't ready to say that out loud yet. His brow was warm and soft as she brushed a patch of silver hair out of his eyes. The musculature of his face had been affected by the stroke. He didn't look the same, but he was still her daddy.

"Anyway, we left Sunshine at home with Aibileen for the morning. I'll bring her after lunch, if the nurses think you're up for another visit."

Danel's phone buzzed, and he pulled it out of his pocket and replied to the text. "Sorry, luv. Enjoy your time together, I'll step out in the hall."

She shook her head. "Don't be silly. Bring him in and close the door. You can't be talking daemons and Hell Realms in the corridor of a busy hospital. Besides, I haven't seen Kang since—"

"Since I saved your scrawny ass a year ago. Yet still you picked this asshole over me."

Ronnie got up and met the Atlanta garrison commander with a hug. Asian-born, built, and brawny, Kang wore the same dark, brooding look of worry all the warriors did. He might stand considerably shorter, but she knew first-hand he was no less deadly.

Kang hugged her, holding her in his arms as he spoke against her ear. "I'm sorry to hear about your father, Ronnie. He's a good man and has done a lot for this city."

She rubbed his muscled back and fought off the emotion

pushing up on the back of her throat. As much as she appreciated the support, she couldn't talk about him yet.

Pulling back, she smiled. "No wings? Haven't been able to replace me, I see."

He winked and kissed her cheek. "You are a rose beyond compare, my sweet. How is a male to find another so rare?"

"All right," Danel said, pulling him back and rolling his eyes. "Enough of the southern charm. She's taken."

"Very, very taken," Ronnie said, nodding.

"By a big brute who doesn't share well with others."

Ronnie leaned to the side to see who came in the room and spoke. "Bentley?" She rushed over and gave him a hug. "It's been ages. How are you?"

Bentley kissed her forehead and pulled her into a side hug. "Didn't your watchdog tell you? I came by to check on you last night, and he promptly showed me the door."

Danel straightened, crossing his arms over his thickly muscled chest. "And if I catch you snooping around in our daughter's bedroom again, you'll get more than an escort to the front porch. Consider yourself warned."

Oh dear. Ronnie pulled out of Bentley's hold and pressed her hand to Danel's cheek. He turned, as usual, to kiss the tender flesh of her palm. "You go figure out how to save the world. I'll be over here catching up with an old friend."

Danel scowled. "You sure you don't want me to throw him through the window?"

She chuckled. "I love you, broody man."

Danel gave Bentley the universal "I'm watching you" signal by pointing to his own eyes and then pointing at out at his. She would've laughed if she didn't know how dangerous a mated dark angel could be.

She waited while Danel, Kang, and another warrior who came in carrying a duffle of books, settled at the sitting area in the corner. It was impossible for her to believe there could be a second man like Danel—an archivist, historian, and linguist.

"I'm a walking, talking, Rosetta Stone," he'd told her when they were first finding each other. *"Our proclivities come from our sire. Gabriel has certain strengths as an Archangel, and as his bastard offspring, I have certain gifts."*

She eyed her husband's counterpart here in Atlanta.

Was he the offspring of Gabriel too? His eyes weren't the warm caramel-gold of Danel and Ringo's, so she thought not.

Still, she wondered what he—

"I never pictured you falling for a brute, Nica," Bentley said, watching her watch Danel. "With your conviction to help people, and your intelligence, I always figured we'd end up together someday."

Her gaze shot from Bentley to Danel sitting twenty feet away, and cringed. Even with her husband deep in a hushed conversation, she knew him well enough to know his attention would be focused on her—well, Bentley more than her.

She didn't want to leave any opportunity for him to get close to her, so she resumed her place at her daddy's bedside.

"You look amazing, by the way. Strong. Healthy. Howton mentioned that you're in remission, but my lord, the difference is staggering. You're as pretty as a peach, Nica Rose."

The low growl rumbling through the room could've been explained away as a mechanical noise from a vent or a distant machine if she didn't know it was her husband.

But she did know, and she knew Bentley's presence was quickly wearing thin. "So, you came by last night?"

Bentley rounded the opposite side of the bed and nodded. "I picked up some foundation files of your father's and wanted to talk to you about your intentions. If I overstepped by coming up to knock on your door, I apologize. I didn't realize I'd be met by such a hostile front."

Ronnie sighed, annoyed Danel would take it upon himself to

beat Bentley off with a stick, but not willing to air that in public with his brothers-in-arms there too. "I was not fit company last night, I'm afraid. Danel acted in my best interest and gave me the seclusion I needed. Don't take it personally."

Bentley didn't look convinced. He pushed the bridge of his glasses up, and she realized they weren't prescription. When had he become invested in his image? The boy she knew in school was content standing on his own merits.

"Tell me now," she said, trying once more. "What did you want to talk about?"

Bentley leaned back and crossed his ankle over his opposite knee. Pursing his lips, he picked an invisible piece of lint off his argyle sock. "Howton took me on as his personal counsel after you went off on your adventure several years ago. Your father had plans in place on how he wanted his affairs handled should his life come to an unexpected end, and the responsibilities you are to assume."

She raised a brow. "Really. You two good ole boys have things all worked out, do you? Do I get a say in any of it?"

Bentley shrugged. "He knew you'd want to carry on his work since everything he ever did was a sacrifice for you and those who suffer as you do."

The tightening of her father's fingers around her hand scared the stuffing out of her. She gasped, and Danel was with her in the next heartbeat. "What is it?"

"He squeezed my finger."

Danel hugged her from behind and rubbed her arms. "He knows you're here for him, baby. He may not be able to communicate it, but he knows."

"Perhaps he heard our conversation and wants you to hear me out. The Hennington Foundation was built for you, after all. It falls to you to keep his efforts alive."

Was that what it was?

The nurse said that despite involuntary movement, the man

she knew as her father was gone. Her heart ached to believe him clutching her finger meant more.

Maybe her daddy *did* want her to hear Bentley out.

She squeezed Danel's arm and pointed back to the seating area. "Sorry, I didn't mean to interrupt. You go back to your meeting. I'm fine here."

~

Zander jogged down the sweeping staircase to the foyer and pressed his fingers to his tongue. Letting off a shrill whistle, he waited for the sound of heavy footsteps to head his way. "Gear up and get ready to move out, my brothers." His men filed out of the war room and met him while he buckled his boots. "If you need it, get it now 'cause we're outtie. Danel, Kang, and Michelangelo confirmed this is Asmodeus, and they have an educated guess on how to break him from his task."

Brennus pushed to the front of the pack. The tension in the Celt's frame had him wondering how he hadn't seen something this obvious growing right under his nose? His brother was invested in Colt's well-being—heavily invested. "How do we get him out of this, Z?"

Zander hoped they could, for all their sakes, but especially for Brennus's. "A blood sacrifice put Asmodeus on Colt's trail. Blood from the same summoner is how to call him off."

"Do we know who that bastard is?" Brennus asked.

Seth nodded, and finished lacing up his red Doc Martins. "Yep. That bastard would be his dickless cousin Andz'gar, the royal Ice King."

Brennus cursed and shook his head. "He summoned a greater demon to take out his own kin? That's fucking low."

"Yeah, it is," Zander agreed. "So, we have no problem kidnapping him and making him bleed when the time comes."

Brennus's smile was cold. "No problem at all."

Zander looked to Bo. "Any word from your female?"

"Yeah," he said, pulling out his phone and calling up a screen. "Andz'gar will be at his office on Wellington until two o'clock this afternoon. He has two building security onsite, as well as four private security and his secretary."

He read out the address and the men nodded in turn. "Lock and load, my brothers. Let's go kidnap a king."

CHAPTER TEN

*T*hree. Two. One. As Brennus dropped his last finger on the count, he led the charge on the assault and reined his beast in the best he could. Blood drawn here wouldn't soothe the burn of his soul. They needed Andz'gar alive, at least for a few more hours. Then all bets were off. The insurgence brought them in from all angles, the king's office on the second floor of a three-story brick building.

Bo and Hark rushed through the front door, taking out the office security. The twins and Zander made quick work of the bodyguards, while he and Kyrian went in hard at the king.

Most Darkworld species heads could hold their own in the bare-knuckle nad-mash of politics as well as the dark shadows of back rooms.

Andz'gar was no exception.

The Ice Demon king met their invasion into his space with hostile force, his knife skills wicked dangerous—even more so because the fucker came at him with dual red-metal blades.

"So ye joined the rebels, have ye?" Brennus evaded the swipe of the bleeding edge and cursed. "Yer makin' things worse fer yerself, dickwad. Come quietly, and it'll be over quicker."

The fucker didn't seem to agree.

Coming strong, the king tackled him to the carpeted floor of his office. They landed in a tangle of elbows and knees, grunting and wrestling for control of the knives.

Brennus pulled back and palm-thrusted. The meaty crack of cartilage rewarded his effort, and he took pleasure in the male's pain. "Stop fussin'. Yer helpin' us get him back, whether ye like it or not."

"I think it's a *not*, Celt." Kyrian stood watch, giving him the honor of working off steam.

Brennus feigned to one side, and when Andz'gar took the bait, he pinned the king's hand and yanked back. The snap of bone brought a bellow of fury.

"My *arm*."

With one knife abandoned, he shot the asshole's other arm, and the battle was won. Brennus's chest burned, oxygen coming in hard pulls. He hauled Andz'gar to his feet and exhaled. "Ye sorry sac-o-shite, ye bound yer own kin to a greater demon, and we'll see that ye pay for it."

Andz'gar spat at him, twisting as if he still had fight in him. "I was forced to save face with my people. I know about you two, Watcher. What will the Darkworld think? What will your beloved brothers think?"

Kyrian flared his wings and stepped in fast. "His brothers stand behind their own, asshole. Private lives are just that— private. Loyalty is more important than saving face. Where's your fucking family honor?"

They met the others in the front office, and Phoenix opened a portal. As the space before them burst into a vortex of energy, Brennus drew a steadying breath. If Storme pinpointed his blood in Hell successfully, this might well be over soon.

Hang on, cop. I'm coming.

The beauty of portals is that they take you precisely where

you want to go. Without a gate at the opposite end, the conjurer focuses on a person, or place, and that's where you emerge.

As their hunting party stepped through the passageway, Brennus thought it was a good thing too, because by the feel of Colt's energy, the cop didn't have a moment to waste.

"What are we looking at?" Seth asked.

Brennus's eyes and mind flat-out didn't understand what they were seeing. He couldn't possibly be looking at . . . but fuck, yeah, it was.

Right in front of them, hanging on chains bolted into the ceiling of a cavern, was a mass of flies crawling, and buzzing, and teeming over one another.

"What the fuck is that?" Zander said, the planes of his harsh face sharp with disgust.

Brennus reached out with his gift, and his bowels twisted. Colt's energy registered weak, but there was a trace. "Colt," he moaned. "Sweet Lady, no."

"You're saying he's under the swarm?" Bo pointed to the pulsing horde of small bodies and cupped a hand over his mouth, either to stop a scream or vomit, he wasn't sure which.

Brennus gave the base of the bug pod a gentle kick to make the horde fly off. "Yep. I see his feet."

"Well, I'll never sleep again," Seth said, rushing over to help. The disturbed flies about-faced and rejoined the masses. "How do we get them to stay off?"

Phoenix raised his hands, and the energy in the air soured. The hair on the back of Brennus's neck stood on end, and the flies began to disperse.

"You're a living Raid, my brother," Seth said. "So many hidden talents."

Brennus ignored the Peanut Gallery, and lurched to examine what was left of Colton Creed. What the feasting pests left behind made him sick.

The male jerked, and the movement was a relief.

"Help me cut him down." Brennus drew his dagger and fought not to gag. The male had been tortured to within an inch of his life. His skin hung off him in bloody ribbons, his body covered in piss, vomit, and maggots. With his face swollen so badly, if they hadn't tracked Colt there by his own blood, he wouldn't be sure it was him.

"S'all good now, cop," Bo said, his voice rough with emotion. "We've come to take you home."

"No. You've come to die," a horrible voice crooned from the mouth of the cavern. "That is my plaything."

Zander, Phoenix, Hark, and Seth positioned themselves between Colt and Asmodeus, while he, Kyrian, and Bo worked to free him from his bindings.

Once they laid him on the dirt floor, Kyrian dropped to his knees, and started healing him. "Give me all the time you can, my brothers. I need it."

While Kyrian worked, Brennus picked maggots from Colt's flesh and fought not to break down. Honestly, they each told the other that getting together was a bad idea, but he never imagined this.

He expected backlash, opinion, and disapproval.

This was barbaric.

He paid no attention to what Zander and the others were doing behind him but remained distantly aware they were offering up Andz'gar's blood to break the contract. He didn't seem to be cooperating, so his brothers were doing a little torturing of their own.

Good. He hoped the bastard held out until they bled him near death.

"His lung was punctured," Kyrian said, his face drawn. "I don't know how long his body was deprived of oxygen. He certainly couldn't breathe with those flies on him."

Brennus cursed.

A tingle crawled up his neck for the second time and he

looked around. Someone else was crashing the party. The air emitted a powerful electrical charge as an ebony-haired male materialized.

Thank fuck. He'd take the Dark Prince over Asmodeus's fellow greater demons any night of the week. "Shayton, have ye come to help or hinder?"

Shayton, Prince of Hell, was a lean, athletic male with long, silky hair, and the fine features of an aristocrat. He shared the same ethereal beauty as his sister, but he wasn't the Prince of Hell for nothing.

He was wily and more dangerous than any other.

The male smiled and gave him an appreciative nod. "Allo, mate. In truth, I'm bored of doing bugger all and came to bodge this cock up. Although, it seems Zander's got things nailed down." Shayton snorted as Andz'gar squirmed and the Sumerian twisted the knife in his leg.

"Call off your dog, asshole," Zander snapped. "I swear I'll kill you. Remember the Shadow Caster King? Any chance you want to be fried alive?"

"You can't do that," Colt's bastard cousin spat. "I did nothing wrong. I have every right to protect what's mine."

"Aw, shut your crap-flap, Andy," the Dark Prince said, rounding the warriors to join the negotiations. "You know the rules. You pooch it, no one carries you. You fucked over your family, and Z and the boys did their homework. They offered your blood to break the summoning of the greater demon, and on behalf of all daemons, I accept. Contract ended."

"My lord," Andz'gar sputtered. "I did nothing wrong."

Shayton leaned in, the electrical charge in the air amping up twenty-fold. "You fucked one of your own because he's got bigger balls than you."

Andz'gar sputtered, and blood dripped down his chin. "He fornicated with that filthy Watcher—the enemy—and tried to influence me to join them. That's why I did it. He betrayed me."

Shayton raised his hand as if he were about to snap his fingers, and Andz'gar stilled. "You forget who you're speaking to, fuck-nut. I've watched you screw anything that moves at my parties. We both know this is personal. You're afraid of him. Shall we tell the good warriors here why?"

Andz'gar looked at the group of them and scowled. "Fine. I release the contract. Brar'don is free from Asmodeus, but he's still banished from the Ice Demons."

Shayton shrugged. "Fair enough. Watchers, I'll see you safe home. Brennus and Colt are my guests while he mends."

With that, he flicked his wrist and they all disappeared.

∾

Colt was fucked. There was an old saying with his people that translated loosely into "Live hard and die horribly." Yep. He did that—in spades. Hanging by his wrists like a glorified hunting kill, in piss-stained pants, suffocating both from within and because of the swarm of flies clogging his nose, he figured that even though Andz'gar hadn't ordered his death, the fucker had gotten a two-fer.

"Wake up, demon," a male said, both inside his head and out. "You're not dead."

Colt opened what he could of his eyes, and out of the sliver of a crack on his right eye, found the Dark Prince of the Hell Realm looking down at him. That didn't convince him he wasn't dead—on the contrary.

It proved the likelihood that he was.

Shayton snorted. "Honestly, demon. If shit could take a shit, it still wouldn't look as shitty as you, but you're not dead." He leaned down as if to poke him and shoved his finger through his sternum, wiggling it between his ribs.

Colt gasped and lurched to the side, fell off whatever he'd been lying on, and crashed onto the polished marble floor. He didn't mind the pain in his knees, or that his molars rattled. He was too busy being grateful to draw air into his lungs.

"See. Not dead," the Dark Prince said. "You're my guest until you're well enough to head home, or until you want to head home. You can stay. That's cool too."

Colt sat back on his heels, the opulent suite spinning around him at a steady clip. He used the sliver of sight to take in the massive fireplace casting golden light across highly polished marble floors, the black satin sheets on a bed that could comfortably sleep ten, the bar station that rivaled the stock and selection of the RedRum.

All this for him? "You honor me, sire."

"Meh. I owed the Watchers a win for the Viking getting tagged at my party. I hate owing anyone anything. Now, they can call me Even Steven."

He waved his hand and headed for the door.

Shirtless and wearing a black-and-gold sarong tied low on slim hips, Colt saw what all the fuss was about. The Dark Prince possessed the resplendent beauty of the Heavens, the lean strength of a male that worked out on the regular, and that long black hair swishing across his mid-back was killer sexy.

He'd be one hell of a wild ride.

The Dark Prince threw his head back and laughed. "Man, I love daemons. One breath away from death and they're still horny as fuck."

"Maybe I should leave ye to it then, and come back."

Colt tilted his head from where he ass-planted on the floor and caught the russet red hair of his favorite warrior. His heart proved to him that it was, in fact, still beating.

"Hey, Red. I didn't know you were here."

Brennus closed the distance between them and helped him to his feet. "I led the cavalry for yer rescue, but it seems I might not be the knight to win yer heart. The way ye were starin' at Shayton's ass, maybe I misread things."

Colt's heart jolted, and he met the warrior's gaze. Brennus's mouth quirked at one side, and Colt let out a heavy breath. "You're harassing me? I'm beat to shit, and you're playing me and yanking my chain?"

"A guy's gotta right to know where he stands."

Colt rolled his eyes but regretted it. The pain that shot through his skull nearly laid him flat out. He dropped his head and waited for his vision to clear, gripping the strong arms of his savior. "You are exactly the knight I want. It's just that . . . I thought . . . when I blew you off . . . and then you—"

"Stop yer stammerin' and let's get you cleaned up. I ran a warm bath, and Shayton's pixie healer sprinkled her wee herbs and oils in to help with the bites and the itch and such. Yer a fair bit chewed up, and that cannae feel good."

No, it didn't. It felt like his skin was crawling, and the bites and welts itched like his flesh was on fire.

Brennus turned him, and they started a flat-foot shuffle toward the arched doorway across the room. After a year of getting nowhere, he cursed how far the washroom was.

The bed, however, was soooo close. "Maybe I could lay down a bit first. I'm really fucking tired."

"If ye leaned on me, ye wouldn't be wearin' yerself out."

Colt wasn't one to lean on anyone, figuratively or literally. Especially not his ex, who moved on the next day to another guy. Was he technically his ex? Did you have to be a couple before you could call it quits?

"Leave me, Celt. I'm fine here until I regain my strength and catch my second wind."

"In the mighty words of the Dark Prince, shut yer crap-trap, or maybe it was crap-flap." Brennus cursed and bent, swiped under his knees, and lifted him against his broad chest. "If ye'll not lean on me, ye give me no option but to carry ye."

Normally, Colt would've protested being the female in this

sweep-you-off-your-feet scenario, but the room was spinning, and try as he might, he couldn't bring himself to man up.

Brennus knew how bad it was when Colt sagged against his shoulder and allowed the carry into the marble enclave to happen. The cop wasn't that kind of male. It broke his cold, dark heart to see him torn down like this—and it pissed him off royally that it came at the hand of his kin.

"What's the growling for, B?"

"Nothin'," he said, setting Colt on his feet against the vanity. He assured himself the guy wouldn't ass-over-end, and grabbed a stack of towels from the rack. "It's not right, is all."

Colt used the edge of the vanity to shuffle to the toilet. After he took a piss, he met him with a grave face and nodded. "You're right. You shouldn't have to deal with this."

Brennus recoiled. "What the fuck does that mean? I'm here because I chose to be. Well, I would have, if Shayton gave me a choice."

Colt's sad eyes lacked the stunning turquoise light they usually held. "I smell your guilt and regret. It's not your fault, and not your responsibility. This is all on me and Andz'gar."

"Yer cousin is a fuckwad, no argument, but he didnae simply decide to condemn ye to Hell fer nothin'. I was half of that reason, and fer that and yer sufferin', I am verra sorry."

Colt turned his back and took the long way around the tub before attempting to step in. Brennus caught him by the elbow when he tipped and held him steady until he eased into the deep lounger tub.

"I don't take pity."

"Then we're good, 'cause I'm not givin' ye any."

He pegged him with a glare, and Brennus was surprised at the level of anger there.

"Fine. I feel guilty. You were drunk in that alley because of me. Yer cousin did what he did because of me. I'm not the kind of man who'd walk away and leave ye to handle the fallout on yer own."

Colt sank low into the water and closed his swollen eyes. "If you know about the alley, you know I was spying on you and your Hollywood boy-toy. How pathetic do you think that makes me feel? Add the betrayal of my cousin, and what was done to me, I'm not sure I can take any more. Leave me the fuck alone, Brennus. Please."

He saw the quake in Colt's bottom lip and smelled the fall-apart barreling in on them. "I'm sorry. No. Ye pushed me away twice and I'll not be shut out again."

Colt swiped a tidal wave of water at him. "Leave me one shred of dignity. For fuck's sake, you found me covered in my own *shit!* Get the fuck out."

Brennus turned to the glistening gold sinks as Colt's sobs began. He had no idea how to make this better for him. Would him walking out accomplish that? To let him think he thought less of him because of what was done to him?

He didn't think so.

Instead, he shucked off his Watcher's vest and unstrapped his shoulder holster. Setting his weapons on the vanity, he reached behind his neck and pulled his shirt over his head.

"How many times, living as a Celt soldier, do ye think I went into battle? Twenty? Fifty? I cannae say for certain, but there were many. The Highland battles against the British, running the Scottish Companies in the Americas, also again against the British. Anyway, there were many."

He undid his boots, pulled off his socks, and let his pants pool to the floor. He left his boxers on because this wasn't that, and he didn't want there to be any confusion on either side.

Stepping to the back of the massive lounger tub, he gave

Colt a shove. "Move up, cop. I'm comin' in there with ye, whether ye like it or not."

His eyes glowed a brilliant blue and Brennus was thrilled to see the Ice Demon rising within. "Why can't you just fuck off and leave me alone?"

"Because I havena finished my story."

He lowered himself in behind his mangled male and spread his legs down each side. When he settled, he pulled Colt's back against his chest and wrapped his arms around him nice and tight. Colt remained stiff and guarded, so Brennus brushed his ear with his lips. He searched for a spot that wasn't red and swollen from his beatings and bites.

"And in every battle, the Scots, the brave men under my command who I loved and respected, wore their kilts. Scared outta their heeds of dying, they charged the enemy, shite running down their bare legs, and nothin' to be done about it."

He pressed his lips to Colt's temple.

"Shite happens, dumbass. I didnae judge them for it then. I willnae judge you fer it now. Now stop being such a stubborn prick and let me comfort ye through this."

"I hate you," Colt said, tears thick in his voice.

"Fer now, ye do, I'm sure, but it willnae last. A part of ye cares fer me too, and that part's a great deal stronger."

CHAPTER ELEVEN

"*R*eally? Brennus and Colt? How did I miss that?"

Zander chuckled at the surprise in Austin's face as the two of them sat on the carpet of their bedroom suite. With their legs out and their socked feet together, they had Nio rolling and revving in her sleeper between them. He helped his baby girl get up on her knees, and she giggled, pumping her legs like she was about to take off across the floor.

"I missed it too. In defense of your match-making prowess, Brennus said it's new. They've never really given it a chance. They just, sort of, collided a few times when things went sideways."

Now it was Austin's turn to chuckle. "Things have gone sideways a lot lately."

Zander nodded. "That's what I said."

"Speaking of that, did you hear from Danel about Ronnie's father? He passed this afternoon."

He picked Niobi up off her face when she tipped forward and sat her on her butt, facing her mama. "I hadn't heard, no. Do we know the arrangements?"

Austin shook her head. "Not yet, but as important as he was, I'm sure it'll be big. Is there any chance we could go and show our support? Atlanta's less than two and a half hours away by plane. We could be there and back before it was time for all y'all to patrol the streets."

Zander thought about that. He'd love to show Ronnie and D the support, but Howton Hennington's funeral would be incredibly public. It had the potential to be an exposure nightmare. "I'll talk to Tanek about it and see what he thinks. Remember, the nine of us are supposed to stay off the radar."

She offered him a soft smile, but it didn't touch the sadness in her eyes. "I understand. I'll send flowers and make a donation to the Cystinosis Foundation on your card."

He shifted onto his knees and crawled over to kiss her. "I'm sure I'll be very generous."

"Naturally. Zander Ambrose is a very generous man." She wrapped her arms around his neck and pulled him down on top of her. His firm, cut muscles welcomed the softness her body offered him. He rolled onto his elbow, caging her beneath him. He pushed up her silky pajama top and ducked his head, kissing his way down the valley of her beautiful breasts.

A rough tug on his hair reminded him they were not alone.

"Da," Nio squealed, bouncing with his hair clutched in her chubby fists. "Da-da-da."

He rolled to the side and included Nio in the love. "I'm sorry, baby girl. Did Daddy forget to snuggle you too?"

～

Danel checked that Sunshine and Rascal were sleeping and closed her door, all but the slightest crack. Heading back across the hall, he shut off the lights and went to Ronnie curled up in front of the fire.

"Is she okay?" Ronnie asked.

"She's perfect," he said, meaning every word. "I bathed her, read her four stories, got her a drink, got Rascal a drink, checked the nightlight, cleared the closet of monsters, and ensured no bad men could get in the windows and take her away."

Ronnie's smile was weak but genuine. "I'm sorry you've been left to pick up all the slack. It's not fair to you—"

Danel dropped to his knees beside her chair and pressed his fingers to her lips. "What do you think these big, strong shoulders are for, if not to carry the weight of the world? It is my honor to care for you two, Ronnie. You and Sunshine are the breath in my lungs, the beat of my heart."

She opened the blanket wrapped around her shoulders, and he scooped her up and settled into the chair with her on his lap. "Lean on me. I'm here for you."

Her tears glistened on her cheeks, catching the dance of the firelight. "Part of me still feels like the girl that needs her mama and daddy. They're gone. All that's left is this big house and the foundation." She gasped as if something struck her and she looked up. "Have you told my mother? Is she still here?"

Danel shook his head. "I searched earlier but didn't find her. There's a good possibility that she was tied to your father, and when he passed, she followed."

Ronnie looked so fragile and lost, it broke his heart. He snuggled her tighter, always mindful of his size and strength, so he didn't hurt her. "How do I make this better for you?"

She curled up against his body, the scent of her tears growing stronger. "Love me."

He wrapped her in his arms and his wings followed suit, cocooning them away from the surrounding world. "Done deal. Consider yourself loved beyond all reason."

They laid there together for a long while before she spoke. "Danel? Can Nephilim transfer garrisons?"

He tilted his head so he could read her face. "Not really.

There are twenty-three doors to the Hell Realm. One on every continent, and a few extra in the cities of first-world countries. That's where the garrisons are and where we are stationed. Why do you ask?"

"This house. My father's foundation. Atlanta is my home. I wondered if transferring to Kang's garrison was an option."

Danel stood and set her back on the chair. "You want me to leave Zander and my brothers?"

"No. I asked a question. I'm thinking."

"You're thinking that we leave our home for you to step into your father's shoes? That doesn't sound like you, Ronnie."

She stared at him and frowned. "Why shouldn't I want to carry on his work? It's the Hennington Foundation, and I'm the only Hennington left."

"You sure that's what it is?"

"What else would it be?"

He scratched his fingers over his goatee and shrugged. "It sounds to me like your fancy-pants Ivy League boyfriend put ideas into your head."

Ronnie rose, her fingers curled into fists. "You think I'm under the spell of Bentley Walker? Give me a little credit."

Danel's beast pulled at his insides. He should've snapped that twig when he found him in Sunshine's room. "He wants you for himself. You see that, right? He thinks he can southern charm his way into your life and lure you back to his arms using family loyalty and grief."

Ronnie chuffed. "You don't think much of me, do you?"

"I think the world of *you*, Ronnie. I also know men like Bentley Walker. He's got the silky bourbon words of a scholar and the bite of a snake. He's working you for some angle, and you're in too much pain to see it."

"Or maybe you're jealous and possessive and get off on feeling like I'm weak. Don't you want me to stand on my own? You like me having a job in the club, where you know where I am, so you and your staff can keep a watchful eye on me. What if *I* want more than that?"

The scent of Ronnie's tears had his beast raging, and his Mark burst gold. Ronnie didn't see his angel side, but she likely could feel the surge of his aggression rising. "If you want more than that, you never said anything, not until Bentley started whispering in your ear. Now you want to walk away from our home, from your friendships with Austin, Storme, and the other wives, from the life we're building? I don't get it."

Ronnie wrapped her arms around herself. "Maybe I miss my roots. Maybe there's more for me here than fitting into your world. *This* is my world, and I like being back in it."

"Do you honestly think that? That I added you to my world like a new gun or leather seats for my Mustang? Fuck, Ronnie, you *are* my world."

"Obviously not, or you would've considered what I want without insulting me and implying I've been brainwashed by a friend."

He tried to reach for her, but she threw up her hands and climbed into the center of the bed.

"Turn off the light as you leave. You can sleep in Sunshine's room or one of the other bedrooms tonight. I'm tired and would like time to myself to think."

∾

Colt lurched up, swiping at his face, gasping for breath. He was suffocating, his skin crawling, his body beaten and blind. He tore at his eyes, fighting to see, trying to remove whatever blocked his vision. Rough hands grabbed his wrists and pushed him back down. He fought harder.

"Calm yerself, cop. I've got ye. Yer safe, here in our bed."

That thick brogue reached through the darkness of his terror. He froze. "Brennus?"

"Aye, it's me. I'm right here with ye in this big comfy bed. I'll not let ye come to harm, I swear it on my life."

"I can't see."

"The swelling's taken hold. This is the worst of it, I promise. From here on, ye'll be on the mend. Deep breaths, demon. Fill yer lungs and know that everything is all right."

Colt did as instructed. The oxygen helped a lot, but what helped more was Brennus's scent thick in his sinuses. He unlocked his muscles and eased back onto the mattress. "Thanks, B. I'm good now."

Brennus rolled him onto his hip, and spooned in behind him. "Yer better, fer sure, but a long way from good. Rest now, cop. I'll not leave yer side until ye can see what life is throwin' at ye. I promise ye that."

He'd take it.

Even if having Brennus with him was temporary, he would accept his company and be thankful. Life would go back to throwing grenades at him soon enough. For now, he had his Celt, and who would've guessed—the male was a cuddler.

~

Andz'gar, King of the Ice Demons, would die. It was a litany of fact thundering through Brennus's mind as he settled Colt back into the sheets and tried to hold the guy together. Beat to shit, snacked on by maggots, strung up to suffocate . . . Every time the cop sank into any dream, the sweats broke loose, and the twitching and groaning came on, like he was reliving it all over again. Yup, the Ice King would pay for this.

The only good thing, if anything, was that Colt's current state made it impossible for him to front and push him away. For the time being, Brennus played the part of the caregiver to his reluctant patient, and the patient didn't have the strength to object. Which was good, because Brennus was wounded too.

Just not on the outside, where people could see it.

He shifted, adjusting the drape of black satin over Colt's hip. This was a new dynamic for the two of them. They'd never lain in a bed together. They hadn't made it past the tearing open of clothes and satisfying the most desperate of urges.

Instantly, Brennus's entire body stiffened. His arousal punched at the front of his boxers, and he eased his hips back off the cop's ass. It was always like that for him with Colt. His skin flushing with heat, his adrenaline pumping as if he were chasing a daemon through the streets, or through the *sheets* as the case may be.

Colton Creed brought out the beast within. That dark and violent side of himself didn't want to mate him. Didn't want to date him. Only wanted the straight-out, hard-core fucking that Colt delivered on. The kind of one-on-one passion that left marks on your skin and filled the hole in your aching heart.

At least, for a little while.

Colt pushed back with his hips and met the solid demand of his cock. "Something on your mind, Celt?"

Brennus cleared his throat and backed up a few more inches. "Sorry about that."

Colt rolled over and tried to look at him, but his eyes were still sealed tight with swelling. "Don't be sorry. You wanting me is the best medicine. Though, I'm assuming it's dark in here because if I look how I feel, I must be fucking roadkill."

Brennus brushed the male's blond hair off his face. It was almost dry from the bath and curling over his ear. He cupped his jaw and brushed his lips with a whisper of a touch. "Aye, it is dark, but the room is kissed with the glow of Hell's flames flickering gold. The ceiling above the bed is mirrored, to show us both here, embraced in black satin sheets. I'll not argue about the roadkill part, but I see ye with my heart, cop. The outside package is temporary."

Colt lay silent in his arms, maybe picturing the image in his own mind, for he smiled a soft, private smile. "The Celt's a snuggler and a sweet-talker. Who knew?"

Brennus chuckled. "Scotsmen take pride in their charms. Gird yer loins, I've barely started."

Colt belted out a laugh, and the sound echoed against all the hard and polished of their guest room. "Did you honestly just tell me to gird my loins? Hilarious."

Brennus chuckled and then ramped it up to laugh. The sensation felt alien and unfamiliar. How long had it been since he'd tipped his head back and laughed?

It felt like a million years.

In the silence that followed, Brennus wondered where he'd gone wrong. In the fifteen years he'd lived with his clan, he'd laughed often and trusted everyone. Unlike many of his brothers, he'd grown up part of something—a family.

At some point, after his Nephilim side activated and he began his training, he'd lost part of himself. It was sad, actually.

The loud rumble of Colt's stomach stirred him from his thoughts. "Are ye hungry, cop? Do ye want me to track down something for ye to eat?"

Colt rolled to face him, and he fought not to curse at the sight. There was no getting used to the brutality. "I *am* hungry, but food isn't what I need to heal. Deplorable creature that I am, I need to feed."

Brennus stiffened and shoved back. "Ye can't keep doing this, cop. Pushing me away and pulling me back. Either ye want me or no. Either I'm a friend or more. I'm not a fuckin' yo-yo."

Colt reached out, his unsteady hand snaking around his neck. "I understand why you don't want to. It was selfish of me to ask, but hey, I'm a demon. Forget it. The Dark Prince will have people around for that—"

The growl that ripped from Brennus's throat was nothing he could contain. He closed his eyes, the pain of this dance driving a spike through his heart. Colt fed on blood. Why hadn't he considered the male needing sustenance to heal? He didn't want to get drawn back in. The cop made his choice. Still, he hated to see him suffer from his wounds.

"When was the last time ye took someone's vein?"

He asked out of morbid curiosity but also to set himself straight. This was a clinical situation of a male needing to eat. He wasn't being asked as a lover. If it weren't him, it would be another—Colt feeding on another, male or female, brought his beast to a rage.

"Jealous, much?"

Brennus bit back a wave of epic anger. "Fuck off and answer the question. Who do I need to kill? When yer well enough, ye can make me a list."

Colt smiled. "The population is safe. I haven't fed since the alley. There's been no one else."

Brennus shifted his hand up and pressed against his heart to reassure himself it wasn't about to burst from his chest. He both loved and hated that answer. He went with the latter and upgraded his frown to a glare, even though Colt was blinded by swelling and couldn't see.

"That was months ago. Why would ye not take better care of yerself? Dammit, cop, no wonder yer layin' here half-dead and sufferin'."

Colt sagged, his injuries and ordeal weighing heavy on him. Now was not the time to lay into the male. Adjusting the pillow behind his head, Brennus eased Colt against his chest and brought his face to his throat. Tilting his head away, he gave him full access. "Take from me, and don't stop until ye've had yer fill. I mean it. I want you strong and healed, so we can have it out on equal footing."

Colt swallowed against the column of his throat, and Brennus could smell the male's hunger. "I can drink from your wrist if it makes you more comfortable. I don't need your throat."

Except, after the horror of them finding Colt hanging in Hell, Brennus needed the body-to-body contact to reassure himself the guy was there and safe. It was going to suck later, but for now, the connection between the two of them would hold him together a bit longer.

"You'll drink from my throat like before."

Colt hesitated, and Brennus was sure he would stall out and back away. This second-guessing would deny him of what Colt needed—of what they both needed.

Brennus gripped the back of his neck and pressed Colt's velvet lips against the pounding pulse of his throat. "Stop thinking and start drinking. Yer pissing me off."

～

Colt gave up trying to do right by his warrior. He climbed onto Brennus's chest and positioned his mouth right where it needed to be. The Celt's skin was hot silk under his lips, and anticipation had the warrior's mighty pulse pumping against his tongue. Colt's fangs dropped in an instant, his body jonesing for what Brennus offered, despite his state of injury.

He licked his lips, parted his mouth, and sank his canines through flesh. Brennus hissed as the richness of his essence flooded Colt's mouth. The first time he'd fed from him, things were wildly out of control, with the fighting and sex and his usual self-destruction going full-tilt toward the edge of the cliff.

This time was different.

Thanks to his wounds, he drank for sustenance and not to get his rocks off. He took his time, enjoyed every sensual nuance. He filed every groan, every brush of the Celt's thumb across his jaw, every breath of lust and devotion into his memory. Later, when he was lonely and cold, he would pull them out and warm himself for a while.

In their few brief clashes, they'd never taken their time. It had always been a frenzy of friction between them. Too much hunger to register where hands were or who rubbed what or why they shouldn't be doing what they did.

This was something else. This was more.

He growled as he gained strength and secured his lock. As much as his mind yearned to mount the Celt and make this about biological need, his body wasn't up for their usual sexcapades. This was a feeding. End of.

That was why he allowed it.

His eyes rolled back in his head as the healing and strength in Brennus's blood took hold. This slow burn wouldn't resurrect the danger which he recently and thoroughly buried.

No reconditioning needed.

This was about healing, rising above his injuries, making himself stronger. It was an isolated and controlled event.

Brennus groaned and rolled his hips. Damn, the guy was rocking one hell of a hard-on. And though the warrior kept things clinical, that wasn't where things were on his side.

With a rough shove, Colt reached between them and pushed the guy's boxers out of his way.

"No, take care of yerself. I'm good."

Colt couldn't speak with his mouth full and wasn't about to stop to set the guy straight. Instead, he wrapped his palm around that thick cock and squeezed.

Brennus bucked in his grip, those heavy thighs clenching, those ripped abs rolling. "But, I suppose, if it makes ye feel better, I could suffer through a bit of fondling."

Colt laughed against his neck and stroked him root to tip, establishing a rhythm.

"Oh, yeah," he gasped, his hips arching toward the ceiling. "Yer fucking gifted, demon."

A lick of pain stung Colt at the term. Yeah, he was a demon, but when Brennus said it, it hurt. It felt like they were different, that their species separated them.

"Are ye all right?" Brennus said, gripping his arm. "Forget me, ye need yer rest."

Colt shook his head and gripped tighter, getting his head back in the game. It didn't matter what Brennus called him—they were different. They were separate.

He focused on his ministrations and it wasn't long before he was tossing the warrior off like a jackhammer gone wild. He reveled in his returning strength. He'd never failed a lover, and he wasn't about to let Brennus be the first.

Brennus's blood held healing magic, and his elevated heart rate gushed blood into his mouth in tidal waves he fought to swallow.

Pumping, pumping, pumping . . .

Brennus came hard, his body going rigid, his breath escaping in a throaty curse, his cock spewing cream in warm, slick spurts over both of them and the sheets.

In the midst of the orgasm, Colt wished he could see. Brennus was beautiful, and not being able to watch him come was a greater punishment than his physical wounds. When the racking spasms subsided, Colt slowed the feeding.

Rocking a light-headed drugging effect from all the blood, he realized how incredible it was that what ran through Brennus's veins wasn't poison to him.

First, it would suck to be poisoned, but second, he'd miss out on the succulence of what it was to take Brennus into his body. Colt growled at his own words.

Take Brennus into his body.

For the first time in his life, he wanted to be dominated by another male. During their encounters, he'd largely been the aggressor.

He'd fucked Brennus.

He'd fed from Brennus.

He'd sucked Brennus off.

He was dominant by nature, and though he'd always been

the male driving the train, with every partner, he would gladly bottom for this male.

I love you, Celt, he thought.

And what do you know? Just acknowledging it in his head was enough to back the semi-truck off his chest and allow him to breathe again. He was right to call it off the other night . . . He was right to want him close now . . . Damn, this relationship stuff was fucking confusing.

Eventually, an internal warning went off, and he realized he had to stop drinking. Brennus, being the male that he was, would allow him to drain him dry. The male was too trusting. He never saw him for who he truly was—a filthy demon.

Despite never wanting to stop, he'd had his fill, and his belly sloshed with the warmth and strength of the warrior. Snaking his tongue out, he brushed over the two injection holes and sealed things up.

"Thank you," he whispered against Brennus's neck. Rolling to the side, the sluggish ten-thousand-pound drag of feeding took hold. "You're a good male, Brennus of Eire."

Too good for him, especially with what was waking inside him. As much as he wished he and the Celt could join the Nephilim team of super lovers, they couldn't.

Too bad deamons don't get a happily-ever-after.

CHAPTER TWELVE

*S*torme's heels *clacked* as she raced through the foyer, grabbed her purse off the glass table of the entrance, and straightened the ivory lilies in the hand-painted porcelain vase. "You have my numbers if you need me. My phone will be on vibrate, but I'll get back to you when I can. The caterers are set on the menu. The linens will be delivered this afternoon. And if there's any chance you can get us a jazz quartet on short notice, I'll give you an extra week's holiday and my undying love."

Jack held her coat up and she shrugged it on. "What happened to the group we already booked?"

She freed her hair from the collar of her jacket and buttoned up. "I didn't get details. The email said two of them were ill and contagious."

Jack's scrunched-up face made her giggle. "Eww, okay. I'll see what I can do."

"You're the best." She blew him a kiss, grabbed her bag, and hurried out the front doors. Jogging in heels was a mistake. She hit a slick spot on the top step and tumbled right into the arms of— "Mr. Logan. Nice catch."

The man set her solidly on her feet and then stepped back. He was a slick man in a suit custom-stitched to fit like a glove. With his hair turning more salt than pepper these days, he wore his age with a distinguished, if not pretentious, air. "Perhaps this demonstration proves my point. Having me around could be an asset. A woman of your age and experience would do well not to rush into breaking ties. You never can tell what might happen if you're taking things on all on your own."

Storme was new to her shifter powers but she was a quick learner, and one of the first things she'd mastered was sorting through the scents people gave off when they spoke.

"You're threatening me?" she said, a sudden bad taste in her mouth. "Let me give you one chance to take that back, because I warn you, I am not on my own, and the people who back me are not the kind you want to piss off."

To punctuate her point, Phoenix strode over from the narrow driveway, his body tight with fury, his eyes practically glowing. Her warrior would have sensed her emotions, and she raised her palm, staving off what could devolve into a horrid mess if things got out of control.

"Let me spell this out for you one last time, Mr. Logan," she said, pleased that Phoenix had reigned himself in. He stood ten feet behind Logan, and the man was so oblivious to his surroundings, he didn't know she likely saved his life.

"Any new Queen Hotel opened will be privately funded and run by me. I no longer have any interest in kowtowing to investors and making others rich. If you want to run a hotel chain, by all means, start your own. I will honor the ownership of those in place, but moving forward, things will change."

Mr. Logan stepped forward, and Storme flashed her husband a warning glare. His Mark had burst into a brilliant neon green, and his beast was at the end of its tether.

I've got this, tough guy. Let me handle him.

"Times may have changed, little girl, but money still talks. I know your net worth, and with the others behind me, we can sink your ship. Try me, and that's what will happen."

Storme wasn't sure if she was supposed to cower or apologize for upsetting the big, rich man, but she wasn't inclined to do either. Instead, she took the offensive.

"Thank you for stopping by, Mr. Logan, but if you'll excuse me, my husband is here to take me to a family event."

She gestured for Phoenix to come forward and fought not to laugh as her aggressive investor stumbled back. As much as Jim Logan thought himself the big man in business, Phoenix was the biggest man she'd ever seen. Over six-and-a-half feet tall, military buzz cut, arms as big as oak trees, he was the mountain to his mole hill.

Mr. Logan wouldn't see his glowing tattoos, but he would see his size and feel his fury arching in the cool, morning air. "Phoenix, this is Mr. Logan, the man I told you about."

Phoenix sneered and spoke directly into her mind. *Can I rip the fucker's head off? Pleeeease? It'll be win-win, promise.*

Storme chuckled and shook her head. "Mr. Logan. As you can see, I'm not alone in life, and Phoenix and I have friends to back us too. I appreciate your interest, but my decision stands. You're out. He's in."

Logan glared between the two of them. "So, what? This strong, silent act is supposed to intimidate me?"

Storme chuckled. "Good grief, no. The strong is nothing he can help—Phoenix is a soldier, and he snaps people in half for a living—and neither is the silent."

Phoenix lifted the leather choker that covered the nasty scar of his youth.

"His voice box was ripped out when he was a child, by his mother of all people. Needless to say, he has anger issues. I actually pity the people who piss him off."

Phoenix tapped his watch, and she nodded. "Like I said, Mr. Logan, you'll have to excuse us. We have family waiting."

~

After Brennus gave Colt what he needed, and vice-versa, the cop fell into a fitful rest of healing, and he decided to get dressed and refuel himself. Stumbling along the fancy, high-polished corridors, numb-limbed and head swirling, he explored the Dark Prince's massive marble temple of opulence.

There must be hundreds of rooms. Who actually lived here? Shayton *annnnnnnd?*

"Hello, Watcher." The Prince of Hell appeared out of nowhere, as if his thoughts called him. Or maybe he simply came around the corner. Who knew?

Shayton had abandoned the silk sarong from earlier and now rocked the wild nakey-wakey, exercising his prerogative in his own home. Yep, he totally got why Colt took notice.

The guy was *puuuurdy*, like a possessive growl in the back of your throat, insta-erection kind of hotness. Silky blue-black hair, a tight body cut and strong in all the right places, and the soft, perfect features of his heavenly birth set him above all other males. Well, next to Colt.

With swagger in his hips, and his mighty V flexing as he sidled over, the Dark Lord fingered the fresh puncture marks on Brennus's throat and smiled. "It seems your lover might have taken too much. How many fingers do you see?"

Brennus focused on the hand in front of him and then looked at the other Shayton with his fingers up too. "Trick question, aye?"

Shayton chuckled. "It wasn't meant to be, but sure, let's go with that. Come. Let's get you something to eat."

With a strong hand at the small of his back, Shayton escorted him into a fancy library and pointed at the velvet fainting couch in the reading nook. "Take a load off."

There was some talking in the background as Brennus flopped and stared up at the endless spines of books standing at attention. The library rose up to a vaulted gold ceiling, an iron spiral staircase at the far wall winding up to a balcony to access the books above. The iron work danced in cables of ebony, while all the gold gleamed like it was polished on the regular.

"Here, drink this."

Brennus accepted the fancy glass and gulped without looking at the contents. "Wow."

Shayton tipped his head. "Thanks for noticing."

Brennus swirled the white wine and watched the refraction of the room dance through the curve of the glass. "I'm a whiskey man myself, but that's good shit."

"That's Chateau Haut Brion Blanc. Yes, it's good shit."

He took another swig and swallowed, liking the burn. Damn, he could drink that like water. "It's got the kick of a pissed-off mule. Hard and fast."

Shayton chuckled and topped him up. "You're a few pints low, Watcher. Enjoy the ride while it lasts."

Brennus drank some more and leaned his head against the velvet arm. With his Nephilim healing ability, it wasn't an easy task for them to get drunk. Apparently, acting the part of a drink box to a daemon beforehand sped up the process.

A servant rushed to the entrance of the library, halting at the threshold as if an invisible barrier blocked his entrance. Shayton met the male, accepted the tray, and sent him on his way. "Chow time, Celt."

Brennus sat up and somehow, instead of lounging on the fainting couch, he now sat upright in a library carrel. He didn't remember relocating but didn't sense being teleported either.

Frowning, he looked around. "Did I do that?"

Shayton's mouth quirked up. "No, I did. You'll feel better after you eat, and in the meantime, I'll find you something to read." He removed the dishes from the tray and set him up.

The succulence of venison stew and colcannon stopped him

from telling the Dark Lord he wasn't much of a reader, his attention now solidly absorbed by the meal.

"This is verra kind of ye, milord." He glanced up as Shayton climbed a rolling ladder, the dimple in his glute hollowing with stunning perfection with the male's movement. "Fuck, ye've got a fine ass."

Shayton chuckled. "Good of you to notice. If your boy wasn't my guest right now, and if I didn't think I'd be a placeholder, we'd explore your interest further."

Brennus's brain was a muddle. Was his comment interest? An offer? Shayton was a stunning male, but he admired him like a priceless masterpiece in a world-class museum. He held great respect for the male's delicate lines and mastery of form, but no heat. Huh. That was new.

In all the centuries, his libido was set on standby, triggered by the slightest inclination or soft breeze.

"Here you are," Shayton said, setting an ornate leather tome down on the mahogany book stand in front of his meal. "I think this particular tale of lore will be of great interest to you."

Straightening, his host patted his shoulder and sauntered off, waving in the air as he left.

And yeah, Brennus enjoyed the view.

Verra much.

Getting back to his meal, he shoveled in more Celtic delight. "Let's see what the good man set out for us, shall we?"

It was a species chronicle written in Enochian. A record of the lives and times of the—keeping his hand in the open pages, he flipped the great leather-bound book to see the front cover —Cryodaemons.

Ice Demons.

Flipping back to the page Shayton opened, he read the title. What. The. Fuck. His blood and booze buzz evaporated in an instant.

The Ascension.

~

Ronnie sat at the front of the church, her hands milling in her lap, her gaze locked on the image of her father in high gloss staring at her from the front. The picture Bentley chose was one of her favorites. It was taken weeks before the car bombing killed her mother. He'd decided to take his clout into politics to make a difference, and he was dressed to impress, driven, and happy with his lot in life.

It was one of the last easy smiles he ever offered the world.

Danel squeezed her shoulder, his arm stretched across the back of the pew, and pressed a kiss to her temple. "I love you."

She didn't want to hear it at that moment. He'd tried to apologize this morning, to talk to her about their fight, but she didn't have the energy. Her father was dead. That was all she had room for in her heart right now.

Giving herself over to emotional exhaustion, she closed her lids and listened to the minister.

". . . about serving the Lord. And now his convictions fall to you. Each and every person sitting here this afternoon has the opportunity to keep Howton's vision and integrity alive."

He sounded like Bentley.

But was that what he would have wanted?

"Howton Hennington led a life of privilege," the minister said, projecting out to the over four hundred people in the church and on the lawns outside. "He had a life most would covet: money, property, and assets a lesser man might have let lead his way. Howton never let his good fortune cloud his responsibility as a son of God."

What? Did this man even know her daddy?

"He understood the importance of giving back. He started the Hennington Foundation to change the lives of those less fortunate, to ease the suffering of those—"

"Pardon me, Reverend. I'll take it from here." Before her

mind registered a thought, Ronnie stood up and climbed the five steps to the pulpit.

The minister sputtered. When it seemed he might refuse to relinquish the spotlight, he glanced over her shoulder. By his reaction, she assumed Danel was behind her, looking violent and intimidating as he always did. The minister bowed his head and stepped aside.

Taking a deep breath, she steeled herself and took the mic.

"Sorry for the disruption, everyone. I couldn't, in good conscience, have Howton rolling over in his grave before we even got him that far, could I, Daddy?"

She glanced to the beautiful rosewood coffin to her right, and smiled at the murmur from the masses.

"For those of us who knew my father, you know he wasn't a religious man serving the Lord. He was a spiritual man who served his family, his community, and what he believed was right and just."

She met Danel's worried gaze and gave him a nod. Her husband sank back onto the first pew and gathered Sunshine into his lap.

"Howton was dedicated. He was driven. He was tough as nails and stubborn as a boulder in the middle of a raging stream. It didn't matter what kind of force you came at him with, he never backed down, and he never yielded."

"Tough as a pine knot," someone called out.

A murmur of amusement rose up from the congregation.

"I see you met him." She looked out at the faces. Many of them she knew from her years here in Atlanta—Aibileen and her family, Jackson and his wife, business colleagues—and many she didn't.

"The minister mentioned Daddy living the life of privilege." She twisted sideways and shook her head. "Sorry, *padre,* that's where you lost me, and if Daddy knew I let that one pass, he'd skin my hide and nail it to the barn door."

"Tell it like it is, baby doll," Aibileen said, winking at her.

"It's no secret Howton married well above his pay grade, but he worked like a dog every day after to earn his place at my mama's side."

"Miss Scarlett was an angel long before she got her wings, Miss Veronica," Jackson said.

"That she was, Jackson," Ronnie said, suddenly struck again with the worry of what her daddy's passing meant for her mama's ghost. Would she follow him to the after?

She met Danel's worried gaze and hated the distance between them. That was on her. They'd both been upset last night, but she'd been the one to shut him out. No. She didn't think he injected her into his life and wanted to keep things status quo.

She looked at Sunshine sitting on his knee. He loved that little girl as fiercely as he loved her. They were building something amazing together, and as much as the foundation meant to her, their family meant much more.

"Daddy taught me so much about life and love and conviction. He absolutely would *not* want me or anyone else to fight for his vision—he'd want us to focus on our *own* vision."

She smiled at Bentley sitting in the first row of the pew to the right and shook her head. "Howton Hennington believed in living hard, loving deep, picking up those who fall in your path, and always standing up to the darkness of the world."

She saw them then, taking up the back two rows on the left. Her family—Danel's brothers, the wives, and the children. They'd come all this way. For her. For them.

Tears swelled, and she clutched her fist over her heart.

Zander rose, as did the other warriors. They too clutched their fists against their big hearts.

"Family is what Daddy stood for, so tonight, everyone speak a little sweeter to those you love. Forgive the misunderstandings. Hug someone who needs it. And think of him kindly now and then. That's all we need to do to honor him."

Danel stood, shifted Sunshine onto his hip, and joined her at the podium. She knew the instant he saw his brothers standing at the back. He cleared his throat, and when he spoke, the quiver in his voice gave him away. "The family has opted to keep the burial service private, but Ronnie and I welcome everyone back to the house for an afternoon of shared memories after two o'clock. There are maps on the tables outside the doors. Thank you all for coming."

∼

Colt laid tangled and sweaty in silk sheets, staring up at the mirror ceiling above. He was overwhelmed and overwrought, at the mercy of emotions he had no business feeling. Ice Demon plus Nephilim assassin didn't equal anything that could survive in sunlight. The male was never supposed to get inside his heart. Remnants of the dream he'd woken from hung heavy in the darkness. Their laughter. Their home. Their future.

Love was the stuff of pure fiction—a feel-good emotion humans invented to avoid feeling alone in a fucked-up world. The only person he counted on was himself, and he'd done all right. He considered himself a pragmatist, a realist.

Some might think him a pessimist, but whatevs.

Despite him catching a case of the feels, Brennus had rescued him from capture and fed him. End. Of. The male was driven by duty and compassion. It was bred into his very DNA to protect the innocent, to fight injustice, and to stand loyally beside a friend in a time of need.

That's what this was for him—nothing more.

He'd seen Brennus with his human. The attraction.

He's simplicity in a complicated world. He's also sweet and a good conversationalist.

134

Colt was none of those things.

Still, as he stared at his reflection above, he couldn't deny the warrior had dropped everything to save his life. Not just with his blood—though his essence strengthened him as sure as an infusion of steel in his veins—but he'd taken on one of the Demon Princes to rescue him.

Stupid fucking Andz'gar.

Anger burned hot inside him, pushing at the confines of his ribs, a pressure in his chest that physically hurt. It would serve Andz'gar right if he accepted what was happening—if he embraced what nature had in store.

He couldn't.

It would ruin everything he worked for, hoped for, and even the things he dared not dream for. Still, it was tempting to stick it to his cousin.

Reaching under the covers, he put his hand on his cock and exhaled. After the feeding, his other appetites came to life with a ferocity that wouldn't be denied. His balls were tight, pre-cum slicking the opening on his crown, his abs flexing.

Even beat to shit and with his skin on fire, a feeding hard-on still demanded to be satisfied.

He ignored the length of his arousal and reached down to the smooth skin at the base. As his breath caught short, and his heart pounded, he pressed his fingers and found the barb.

He never wanted this. He hadn't even known about it until the transformation began in that alley. Now, even after his reconditioning, that fucking barb still hovered in place, waiting for him to forget himself, to give in to the most carnal and animalistic side of himself.

Images of Brennus submitting to his hunger in that alley flooded his mind and mixed with the power rushing through his veins from the feeding. Colt had fought the arousal—and lost.

Getting his groove on, his spine lifted and receded as his mouth fell open, and his fangs descended. Fuck, that felt good.

Closing his eyes, he relived the moment when he'd thrown Brennus against the brick wall and dropped to his knees. The guy had fucked his mouth like a savage and come hard, gasping in heavy pants as Colt swallowed every ounce of his cum.

Colt arched in the bed, moving against his own brutal hold. With a grunt, he twisted to the side, his torso working as he gripped his shaft and worked himself even harder.

An orgasm exploded out of him, memories of bending the Celt over the rails in the horse arena, of being inside him, of the great noise they made as they came, and their grunts echoed in the open space.

His free hand crushed the sheets in his grip, and he dug into the mattress with his heels. Arching off the bed, he kept pumping, kept coming in glorious streams of heat.

When he drained, he fell still, eyes closed, heart pounding. He didn't want to see the state of the sheets. He'd made one helluva mess. If fucking Brennus in his head felt this good, he'd lose his mind if they ever got their timing right and had an actual bed session.

The few sexual collisions they'd had over the past months had been spontaneous. They'd never spent time or done things up right. Good thing, too.

Colt laughed at the irony, though there was nothing funny about it. He had to ensure he never ended up hitting the horizontal with the warrior.

He would never survive it.

CHAPTER THIRTEEN

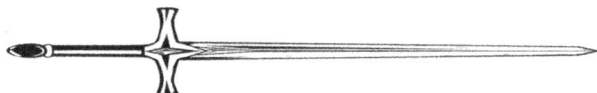

The wheels of the plane touched down, and Zander grimaced at the runway wobble-and-bounce while the pilot steadied their landing. Funny, since he got his wings, he hated flying in planes. There was likely some kind of Freudian theory about him being a control freak, but it was what it was.

As everyone's phones started buzzing and pinging, he flipped his from airplane mode and checked for anything important they missed. It was still daylight, so not much could've gone wrong.

"You did a good thing, angelman," Austin said, leaning against his side. "Today was a good day, considering."

He agreed. Danel and Ronnie were touched the whole gang made the trip. With only Brennus and Tanek absent, they presented one hell of a united front. "This was all you, cowgirl. Every good idea I've ever gotten has come from you first, and everyone on this plane knows it."

Her smile was all the praise he'd ever need in his life. She lit him up when she looked at him like that—like somehow, she thought he hung the moon.

"Ohmygod, Jack?" Storme's voice rose from a grouping of seats a few rows up. "Are you all right? Jack?"

The tone of her voice had him releasing the buckle of his seatbelt and rising to see what was up. Hands shaking, she hit speaker button on her phone and held it up to her mouth. "Jack, answer me. Where are you? What's happening?"

There was nothing on the other end but a wet gurgle he'd heard too many times not to recognize. He'd bet his left one the human couldn't reply because his throat was cut.

"Where is he?"

Kyrian was on the horn to Tanek as Seth jogged up to the cockpit to get the whole taxiing thing locked down.

"I don't know. He didn't say—"

"He's at the hotel," Kyrian said, kissing Cassi before jumping to his feet.

"How can you know that?" Storme blinked up at them.

"We chipped his phone." Zander strode to the door of the plane, then rebounded and caught the look Storme was throwing him. "The kid is near you on a daily basis, so yes, he's on our radar. Sorry, not sorry. End. Of."

"How the fuck do we get off this ride?" Kyrian asked, the plane suddenly getting very crowded with six Nephilim warriors pacing the tiny aisles.

Seth came back and shrugged. "Transport Canada Regulations . . . blah, blah, no chance they'll let us open things up until we're off the runway."

"Fuck that," Zander said, tossing the keys to his Hummer to Taharqa. "Hark and Bo, adjust their memories and get everyone home. Then meet us at the hotel. Ringo, call Drina and get her ready for an incoming patient. Seth, open that door. Now."

"Wait," Storme said, rising. There was no room in the aisle, so she climbed onto her seat. "I'm going with you."

"Hells-to-the-no," Zander said. "There's a time and place to assert your independence, Storme. This ain't it."

"Don't do this, I'm going to—"

"What's that?" he said, leaning closer and cupping his ear. "You're going home with Hark and the others, you say? Fucking awesome. Glad we don't have to waste time arguing."

Zander turned back to Seth and gestured to the door. "I'm waiting, and you know how much I love that shit."

Seth pulled on the door lever, and the thing popped open while alarms sounded. They dematerialized in a rush and were throwing themselves across the city in the next second.

He had no idea what this was about, but their family was like the fucking Musketeers. All for one and one for all.

∿

Brennus sobered up PDQ, his meal solidifying in his gut like a gelatinous stone. His head pounded with prophecies of ascension and the sheer magnitude of the lies Colt stuffed down his gullet. He understood why Andz'gar felt threatened. He *should*. If Colt's weird disappearance was because he'd activated this prophecy, they should all be pissing their pants.

His boots thumped the marble floor, his strides long and driven to get him back to the guest suite.

Colt was fresh out of the shower and looking a fuck-ton healthier. Color in his face. His eyes bright and visible once again. He didn't have a chance to brace himself.

Brennus's fist flew in and cracked him in the face.

The cop did a three-sixty spin and dropped to the floor like a ragdoll. Shaking his head, he got to his knees and prodded his jaw. When he looked up, his eyes were dazed but glowing the most stunning turquoise Brennus had ever seen.

"What the fuck? I like it rough, but a little warning would be nice."

Brennus dropped Shayton's book to the floor at Colt's feet and pointed to the cover. "Yer feeding on me in that alley, we're wild as fuck, and we unleash a fuckin' mythological ice god. How is that somethin' ye fail to mention?"

Colt frowned, opened his mouth, then closed it again.

"Really? Nothin'? Yer playin' the part of a mute guppy blowin' air bubbles at me? Ye had to know yer cousin would lose his mind and come atcha. How did ye think to keep this to yerself? People will notice an eight-foot ice god walkin' the streets of Toronto."

"I know," Colt said, rising unsteadily, his cheek red, his lip bleeding. "Why do you think I left? I went to the ice regions of Hell and had the elders lock me down. Do you think I wanted that? Do you think I enjoyed months of torture? Do you think I, in any way, want to be the Antichrist Superstar."

Brennus ground his molars. "Obviously, I dinnae ken what ye think about much, do I?"

Colt's laugh was harsh, his fingers curled in fists. "I left the ways of my family and my culture behind to build my own life in the Human Realm. I like who I am there. I help people. I have friends. Unlocking Avestaexa is the last thing I want and the last thing I expected."

Brennus pointed at the book. "It says in there that it's in yer family. Ye had to ken it was a possibility."

"No one unlocked his powers in millennia. It's a myth, a bedtime story parents use to scare the crap out of their kids." Colt paced to the tussled sheets of the bed and rebounded like a snapped rubber band. "Of all the Ice Demon's, I'm the least interested in dominating the ice realms of Hell. I don't want to rule. I don't want subservient people bowing at my feet. I don't want any of it."

"What if that's not the only outcome? If ye'd let me in on yer secret, we could've been working on another path. Maybe there's a benevolent option in this somewhere."

Colt stopped dead and threw him a droll stare. "The last time Avestaexa took form, he demanded total dominance over my people and half the Hell Realm. He enslaved them for a thousand years, killing men, fucking their wives, tormenting children. Nothing done could stop him. He only went into hibernation because he got bored waiting for more interesting worlds to conquer. What do you think he'll think of the Human Realm? Him waking up is nothing but bad news."

"Maybe it'll be different this time."

Colt threw his arms open. "Yeah, it will, because I'll hold him at bay. I'll lock things down until he goes back to sleep and never let him take control of this realm or any other."

Brennus frowned. "Do ye think that's possible. Yer talkin' about takin' on a god, aye?"

"Fuck him," Colt said, raising both his middle fingers and waving them around the room. "I disrespectfully decline the offer of divine possession, fuck-you-very-much."

Brennus couldn't blame him. This was a raw deal and a shit thing to happen to anyone, let alone a guy like Colt. Drawing a deep breath, he exhaled his anger and exhaustion. Sinking back, he sat on the foot of the bed and raked his fingers through his hair. "So, when ye tossed me to the side?"

Colt dropped to his knees before him. "It wasn't anything I wanted. It isn't what I want now. It's just . . . everything about us together is *soooo* wild. You reach a part of me that's never been tapped before. As much as I love it"—he looked up at him, and his eyes were alight—"and I do *loooove* it . . . if there's a chance of keeping this from happening, I gotta try."

Brennus exhaled hard, hating this.

He couldn't disagree. At least now, he knew the truth. His life had always been about sacrifice. Nothing new there. "So, we go home and cool things off."

Colt sat back on his heels and looked up at him, his expression pained. "Look on the bright side. I have a slew of dumbass cousins. Maybe one of them might spark Avestaexa's interest, now that he's awake."

Fucking hell. Looking into those blue eyes, those bottomless cerulean blue pools, he wanted there to be another answer, something that didn't draw a line in the sand and leave them sitting on opposite sides.

"If one of them does win the ice god lottery, I expect you to track me down."

"Are you kidding? I'll beat down your door and rip off your leathers before you know what's happening."

Brennus forced a crooked smile. "Ye better text me yer on the way, in case I'm in the living room with the wives."

They both chuckled.

After a moment, Brennus couldn't take the distance between them, even though they sat only inches apart. He opened his arms, and Colt leaned forward and hugged him around the waste. Brennus stroked the cop's hair and kissed the top of his head. "Ye realize ye just gave me the 'it's not you, it's me' speech, aye?"

Colt chuckled against his chest. "I guess I did."

～

Danel walked Ronnie up the steps of her southern plantation home, and guided her to the porch swing. The last of the funeral attendees was driving down the treed lane, the taillights of the car glowing red against the dusk of early evening. The strength his wife possessed never ceased to amaze. Her disease left her petite and frail, but also gave her an iron will and determination.

"Sit with me, my female," he said, pulling her into his lap as the swing sank under his weight. "Let me hold you for a moment before we face the world."

Ronnie sat sideways on his lap, wrapped her arms around him, and rested against his chest. Whatever she'd struggled with seemed to have worked itself out during the funeral. He wanted to ask her about it but wouldn't stir anything up while emotions were so fresh.

"Everything went well, don't you think?"

He nodded and pressed his lips to her ear. "I'm sure your dad appreciated the turnout. He was a well-respected man."

"It was thoughtful for everyone to fly down for the day. I looked to the back of the church and almost broke into tears when I saw Zander and the others."

Yeah. It meant a lot to him too.

He'd never known the love and support of family, until Z and Austin pulled their violent half-lives together like nothing he ever dared dream for.

"Did you know they were coming?"

He shook his head. "I was stunned when I saw them. Z wanted to stay longer, but they had to get back before dark."

"Of course. Being celestial protectors of a city outranks staying to help consume a mountain of southern cooking."

"I've honestly never seen so much food."

Ronnie chuckled. "It's the way of the south. There's no heartache a warm hug, and a good meal, won't make better."

He was glad that's what she was brought up with. With his toe on the porch, he swung them in a gentle arc back and forth, staring out at the sky darkening over her family land. It seemed so peaceful there, but with her mom's car bombing and Ronnie's illness, he supposed nothing held heartache and troubles away completely.

"Can I ask you something?"

Danel gave her a gentle kiss as she pulled back. "Of course."

When her brow creased, he wanted to smooth it out with his thumb, wanted to fix whatever had her looking so serious and pensive. "As a member of the Choir, can you . . . do you have access to those who pass?"

He brushed the side of her cheek. "I'm sorry, luv. That's beyond my scope. Why do you ask?"

She shrugged. "No reason. I'd like to check on him, to know he's all right, to let him know that I'm all right, and he can rest."

"He knows. I'm sure he knows."

"What about Mama? I thought of it again while I was standing at the pulpit. Can you inquire if she's passed and is with him? Gabriel would know."

The thought of asking his deadbeat dad for anything churned his guts, but the worry in his wife's eyes hollowed him out even more. He'd been through the house a dozen times, searching for the ghost of Ronnie's mother. With no trace of Scarlett, he was fairly certain she was bound to Howton and now, with his death, had moved on.

"Of course, luv. I'll see what I can find out."

∾

Phoenix rode the wind to the hotel and materialized in the pitch-dark of the recessed entrance. The door was unlocked, the thick stench of blood polluting the foyer. As Z, Kyrian, and his twin took form and joined him, he found the panel and turned on the lights. He'd worked long enough in this existence to recognize death when he saw it. Jack's eyes were fixed, his body still. Not a moan. Not a gurgle. Not a twitch.

Fuck.

Kyrian went straight for Jack's lifeless shell, Seth and Z outed their weapons and secured the space, and he let himself into the locked room behind registration where Danel set up the security feeds.

It took him the work of a moment to log onto the computer and pull back the tapes. Four men. Human, by the look of them. This wasn't their jurisdiction, which complicated things.

In all things Otherworld, they were the bomb.

In the human world, they abided human laws.

9-1-1, it was.

~

Colt stepped into the station staff room and smiled. Damn, it felt good to be back. He closed his eyes and breathed deep. Aside from the lump of ice lodged in his chest, he almost felt normal. The low drone of phones ringing, the smell of coffee mixed with Jose's Mexican microwave delight, the bump of the tiny paint blob on the handle of his *I Love Big Busts* mug.

Home sweet home.

"Creed," Blakney said, following him into the social hub of the office. The Staff Sergeant seemed in good spirits. Then again, with Colt's return to duty, the guy was off the hook for straight nights. "Welcome back. I thought—what the fuck happened to your face?"

Colt positioned his favorite mug under the coffee dispensing nozzle and selected hazelnut with extra cream. "Would you believe that while I recovered from a demon attack, my ex got pissed and sucker punched me? I've been on one hell of a roll, I tell you."

Blakney rolled his eyes and grabbed a cherry Danish off the plate. "Still a wiseass, I see. Good to have you back, man."

Colt leaned his ass against the counter and lifted his chin. "See you out there."

He waited the few minutes for his java nirvana to drip into his mug, and then took his bounty to his desk. Technically, he wasn't on duty until tomorrow night, but no sense wallowing in an empty apartment wishing things were different, when he could come in and see what he needed to catch up on.

The first thing he noticed was that someone swiped his chair. Looking around, he spotted it and got his thick rubber treads moving. Grabbing the seatback, he wheeled the thing back to his desk, squatter and all.

"Fuck, Creed, what's your problem." Davies starfished as the momentum threw him backward.

"Get off my chair, and there won't be a problem."

Colt ignored the grumble of colorful curses thrown his way and arrived back at his desk with one empty desk chair. After turning on his computer and monitor, he waited for things to boot up. He had weeks of alerts to go through. Watch lists. Shift reports. This would take all night.

Good. That would keep both his mind and libido occupied enough that there wouldn't be any Celtic crossover. Distance. That's all they needed—a little time and a lot of distance.

This too shall pass, right?

It's not like he and Brennus even got off the ground.

They'd never been on a date.

They'd never shared a meal.

Hell, he'd never even gotten a ride in the male's R8.

He rubbed the icy void beneath his sternum and cursed as his memory flooded with high-def images of Brennus picking up that human, looking so fucking sexy in his kilt.

The growl that rumbled out of his chest was nothing a human could make, and the perp at the next desk turned to stare.

"Eyes front, asshole," Colt snapped, getting back to his own business and clearing those pictures from his replay loop.

Yeah, distance. That's what he needed.

"Hey, Creed," Blakney said, holding up his radio. "I've got a silent alarm and a possible DOA at one Queen Hotel. You know the owner, right?"

Colt launched to his feet and grabbed his jacket and phone. "Yeah, Storme's a friend. Tell me she's not the DOA."

"No. It was called in as a twenty-something male."

Colt shoved his arms through the sleeves and woke his phone to check for messages. Twenty-something covered a lot of ground in Toronto and told him absolutely nothing about the identity of their victim. "Who called it in?"

"Some guy . . . Amber . . . Ambro."

"Ambrose," he said, breathing a huge sigh of relief. If Zander called it in, it wasn't one of his, or they'd handle it in-house. "Zander Ambrose."

"Another friend?"

"Yep. He's solid. Ex-military. Owns the O-Zone nightclub and funds half the soup kitchens and hostels in the city. A good guy who tries to make a difference."

They slid into Blakney's car and were on the scene in less than four minutes. They parked to one side of the lane that led to the parking lot behind the building and approached the front doors shoulder to shoulder.

Zander, Phoenix, and Kyrian milled around the front entrance, smoking the Greek's imported fancy tobacco. Colt caught himself looking around.

Was he hoping to catch a glimpse of Brennus? What was he just saying about needing distance?

The lights in the hotel lobby illuminated the scene inside. The place was bloody, but after some of the scenes he worked with the garrison, this was sadly ordinary: a glass table smashed in the entrance, some flowers and broken ceramic shards on the polished tile, and a body.

"Staff Sergeant Blakney," Colt said, joining the three and pointing them out in turn. "This is Zander, Kyrian, and Phoenix. Storme Queen, the owner of the hotel, is Phoenix's wife."

Blakney looked at the three of them, and Colt knew the Watchers would sense his sudden trepidation. Nephilim were built to intimidate, and even though Blakney was human and couldn't see their Marks or their seven-foot ebony wings rising up behind their heads, he had keen instincts and would sense their violent power held in reserve.

"I mentioned ex-military, remember," he said, trying to give Blakney something to focus on. It didn't matter anyway because he was now staring at the blood on Kyrian's hands and the white cuffs of his dress shirt.

"I'm a field medic," Kyrian said, answering the question before it was asked. "I tried my best when we found him, but he was already gone."

"Did you disturb the scene?"

Kyrian shook his head. "No, sir. I shifted the victim from his side onto his back to work on him, but other than that, the only things we touched were the alarm pad and the lights."

Blakney went inside, felt for a pulse, and then called it in. When he came back out, he had his notepad and pen in hand. "Okay, boys, walk me through this from the top."

CHAPTER FOURTEEN

*B*rennus arrived into an eerily quiet home and wondered what he missed. "Helloooo in the house. Anyone here?" He listened to the hum of the furnace and opted not to take his boots off. Instead, he searched the main floor. The kitchen was the hub of things, so he started there. "Hello? Where is everyone?"

Finding nothing and no one in the kitchen, he pulled out his phone, a rising panic drumming through his veins.

"I don't care!" Storme shouted, back at the front entrance.

Brennus retraced his steps and met Bo and Hark bringing the wives and children up from the tunnel. By the look of them, he missed a family road trip—oh, and Storme was pissed.

"What's going on, lass? Why has ye so wound?"

"Brennus, thank the goddess you're home." Storme rushed to hug him. When she peeled back, he noticed her usually rich mocha skin was awfully pale. "Something happened to Jack, and they won't let me go to the hotel!"

He looked to Bo and Hark. "What happened?"

They frowned and glanced to the women. Brennus's beast burst forward. "I'm not in the mood, lads. Dinnae treat the ladies like delicate flowers. They know well what evils the world holds and what we face each night. Now spill it."

Bo raked a hand through his long, blond hair and cursed. "Jack's dead."

Storme gasped and he grabbed her around the waist to keep her standing—to keep them both standing.

"Phoenix doesn't want Storme there until they get things cleaned up. He doesn't want her reminded of a bloody scene every time she walks into her hotel."

"When?" Brennus snapped. "How?"

"Moments ago, in the hotel lobby. Kyrian tried to keep him breathing but arrived too late."

"Who?"

"Seth and Tanek are working on that."

"*I* can tell you who's responsible," Storme snapped, patting his arm and straightening. "For shit's sake, tell Seth to track down Jim Logan. He's the lead shareholder in Queen, next to me, and he's been threatening me for weeks."

Bo frowned. "Does Phoenix know that?"

"Of course not," Storme said, looking at the Viking like he was an idiot. "Would you tell Layne every time a hothead spouted off at you? Would you have her angry and worried for nothing?"

"Not for nothing, lass," Brennus joined in. "If Jacky's dead, the bastard is more than a hothead."

"He's not dead. He can't be." Storme brushed her brown curls away from her face, her hands trembling. "Look, boys, it's my hotel, and I need to get there. Do you two remember what happened the last time you kept me from something?"

Brennus looked at Hark and cursed. They did.

The two of them were knocked unconscious for almost two days. "Aye, all right. Hark, you drive her over. Bo and I will go ahead, let Phoenix know, and we'll call if there's going to be a major problem."

He looked at Hark and raised his hands. *Drive slowly, my brother. As slowly as you can get away with.*

Brennus and Bo jogged out to the racetrack oval and flew straight up into the cover of the darkness. Above the streetlights and the city's ambient glow, they moved unseen and were at the hotel in minutes. They landed at the back and came around to find Z, Kyrian, and Phoenix laying things out with a silver-haired cop.

An ambulance drove up and parked, its lights twirling but no siren on. Jack was dead.

Guilt festered like a septic wound in his heart. Maybe if he'd been there, he could have stopped this. Maybe if they'd been dating proper, Jack wouldn't have been alone.

Maybe. Maybe. Maybe.

Brennus didn't bother to stop and talk, he went straight inside and to the fallen man. He fell to his knees on the hard, blue tiles and took in the stuff of nightmares. Jack's throat was slashed wide, his soft gaze now fixed and unseeing.

"Oh, Jacky boy, I'm so verra sorry."

He thought about their parting a few nights ago. Jack, so full of life and understanding. So young and full of potential.

"I'm sorry, Celt."

Brennus pulled from the fog of his mind and lost himself in the blue stare that met his. Sincere. Suffering along with him. Colt squatted down on the opposite side of the body and frowned. "Take your time, but don't touch anything, 'kay? Human's have their way of doing things."

Brennus sat on his heels and rubbed the back of his neck. "We planned to go for Korean barbeque this weekend. As friends, but I looked forward to it. He was a quick wit, this one." He caught the pain in Colt's expression. "I'm sorry, cop. That was thoughtless."

Colt shrugged. "Don't sweat it. It is what it is, right? This is where we are."

The crunch of glass signaled the arrival of the ambulance attendants and the stretcher they rolled in. Brennus stood up and backed away. "Storme's coming with Hark. Can ye warn Z and Phoenix there's no stopping her?"

Colt nodded. "I'll try to divert her through a side door and find somewhere quiet to take her statement. That way she won't have to—"

A heaving gasp had them both jumping. They turned to see Jack sputter, choke, and spit up blood. Brennus dropped to the floor and got in front of those panicked eyes. "I'm here, Jacky. Hang on."

"Shit, get in there, boys." Colt jumped back while the paramedics grabbed their bags and took over.

Brennus got out of their way and everything kicked into high gear. Hands flying, tubes getting shoved, humans calling out numbers, and recording things.

"What the fuck was that?" Brennus asked, his heart pounding as he and Colt shuffled even further out of the way. "That boy had no vitals and was going cold."

Colt shook his head. "Don't look at me. I don't have the juice to bring someone back."

Well, someone did.

Brennus watched the humans working on Jack and found his chest warming with the spark of hope.

Please, sweet Lady, if it be yer will. Jack is a kind soul and a good man. Help him survive this.

~

Colt jogged alongside the paramedics as they transferred Brennus's human to the ambulance. The kid coded once in the lobby after they got him strapped on the gurney. They weren't sure how he remained alive. Now, wound dressed, intubated, and bagged for oxygen, he seemed to be refusing to die.

Good. That was good.

Even though, to the very depths of his cold, dark soul, he hated the idea of Brennus caring for another man, he also didn't want the kid dead, or Brennus would wear that badge of guilt and regret for the rest of his life.

The Celt was too big-hearted not to.

Hark pulled up and parked Storme's white Mercedes in the now congested driveway of the hotel. Phoenix's female jumped out of the car and ran straight toward the back of the ambulance. Phoenix, Kyrian, and Zander strode over to greet her. She glared, throwing her hand up and the three flew back onto their asses as if they'd been hit by an invisible bat of energy.

Allriiiighty then. Storme was pissed.

"I'm Jack's boss and the closest he has to family," she said, sliding past one of the paramedics to take a seat. Leaning forward, she grabbed Jack's hand. "I'm here, Jack. Don't worry about a thing. Everything will be all right."

As the ambulance drove off, siren wailing, Colt joined the group of Nephilim gathering on the concrete walkway. Zander and Phoenix brushed off their asses, looking stunned. Kyrian rocked the dazed and confused. And Bo, being Bo, simply took everything in.

"Honeymoon's over, Egyptian," Hark said, joining them. "Her eyes glowed gold, and she growled the whole way here."

Phoenix beat feet around the back of the building, no doubt to take to the sky and follow Storme to whatever hospital that ambulance ended up at.

"Where's Brennus?" Zander asked.

Colt shrugged. "Likely tracking the ambulance too. He's been dating that kid and is taking it pretty hard." The words brought bile up the back of his throat, and he felt a thick sheet of ice constricting around his heart.

He breathed deep and let the agony all the way in. If not

Jack, it would be someone else. Colt had to face facts. A male like Brennus wouldn't remain single forever.

He made his bed and chose not to have Brennus in it.

The hard lines of Zander's scowl made the Sumerian look more severe than usual. "Dating him? The human? I thought he was with you?"

Colt turned to make a hasty retreat before the inquiries started flying. "Life's complicated, Z. Really. Fucking. Complicated. Brennus is free to date whoever he chooses."

"Yeah? You don't sound too happy about it."

Happy? It was eating him up.

Zander stayed hot on his heels, not letting him gain any distance. Couldn't the guy take a hint?

"Hey," Zander said, dogging him. "You've helped me out enough times for me to return the favor. Tell me what's doin', and maybe I can uncomplicate things."

Colt turned in a rush, his heart hammering, his fingers tingling with the painful burn and tingle of frostbite. "Worry about your own life, Sumerian. Stay out of mine."

Zander's pale blue eyes widened as his wings unfurled behind him. "You sprung a leak, demon. You might want to get control of that."

Colt looked down at the ice covering the ground between them, and Zander's boots now frozen in place. "Fuck me." Colt got moving again. "Really. Fucking. Complicated."

∼

Ronnie was halfway down the stairs when she heard the knock on the front door. Strange. Not only did people normally ring the bell in a house of that size, but it was after ten and well past the hours of polite visits. Knowing what went bump in the night better than most, she didn't simply answer the door. Glancing through the cut glass design on the sidelight, she peered out to see who was on her porch.

Rolling her eyes, she undid the lock and opened things up. "Bentley Walker, what on earth are you doing here at this time of night?"

His lips on hers caught her off guard. Bourbon and cigarettes bombarded her mouth. Pushing on his chest, she twisted out of his grip. There was a moment of traffic jam in her mind when everything suddenly screeched to a halt.

Whoa. Wait. WTF. "You overstep, Bentley."

"No. I don't. You've known my heart since we were kids, Nica, and you took off and married a thug. I have every right to be angry. Under all this Armani and southern charm, I'm as much a man as that hoodlum of yours. If you were that desperate for a rough fuck and to live on the wild side, you should've said something. I can give you that."

"Don't be crude," she said, a trickle of cold fear creeping into her veins. "Things were never like that between us, and you know it. We are friends, only friends."

"Because your daddy had other plans for you. Daddy's gone now, and I control what happens next."

The glint of sadistic pleasure in his eyes had her gauging the distance from him to the sideboard. Since the Serpentine attack last year, her father kept a loaded gun at the door. "You're drunk, Bentley. Today was a hard day for all of us. Go home and sleep it off."

"Not unless you come with me. You're mine now, Nica. I finally have the leverage to secure you in my life."

"Are you threatening me?"

"I have no need for threats. You know how things work. I scratch your back, you suck my cock."

If she hadn't been freaking out, Ronnie would've laughed out loud. Feigning a calm she didn't feel, she strode over to the sideboard and adjusted the hydrangeas in the arrangement. "I'm sorry if you feel I wronged you, Bentley. On my side, I consider you a friend—a sweet, supportive friend."

"Things are different now."

"Yes. I'm happily married."

He laughed. "That brute doesn't know the difference between a shrimp fork and a pitchfork. He'll never fit into our world. What you need is a business-minded gentleman on your arm to help you run the Hennington Foundation. We'll be the next Rockefellers."

She let that grand delusion sink in while he perched his briefcase on the sideboard next to her and opened things up.

"I've prepared everything. All you need to do is sign, and your course will be righted."

She glanced at the document he held and frowned. "I'm not annulling my marriage to Danel. Are you crazy? I *love* him. I love the life we're building with Sunshine and his family. I'm happy, Bentley, happier than I've ever been."

"Don't say that!" Bentley shoved the paperwork at her. "He's a rebellious fling gone wrong—a cancer in your life."

"Danel's not a cancer, he's the cure. He's the reason I'm in remission. He's given me a future. He's devoted and generous, and always puts my needs and my safety first—"

Slap. The contact knocked her to the marble tiles. Her eyes watered, and the right side of her face burned like it was on fire. Bentley loomed over her. She'd seen that possessed wildness before, in the eyes of the daemons that kidnapped her a year ago.

Evil had a look to it, and Bentley had that look.

"Why are you doing this?"

"You will sign the annulment, and you will marry me. I've been more than patient." He gripped her wrist and yanked her off the floor. The pain in her shoulder made her cry out as he pushed her against the sideboard. "I devoted my life to your father and his foundation, to you and your family. Don't you see that?"

He shoved a pen into her trembling hand and then pinned her wrist to the surface. "Sign it."

The ink of the legal words wavered behind the wall of her tears. "Danel will know you forced me to do this. He won't believe it."

Bentley seized the back of her hair and crushed his mouth to her lips once again. He tasted of violence, his breath hot on her face. The sting of him pulling her hair didn't touch the pain in her chest. She couldn't sign Danel away. Even as a charade to appease a crazy man, she couldn't do it.

"He won't have any choice. The law is my domain, Nica. Once you sign, he'll be out of our lives."

Lost in his demented illusion of passion, Bentley's kiss moved to her jaw, and then her neck. Groping hands pulled at her pajama top. She threw the pen and tried to break his hold.

He was too strong.

The foyer spun and her hips hit the sideboard. Bentley's erection thrust against her back. Bile burned her throat, the acid burn pressing hard and fast.

You've got this, Ronnie, Danel's voice said in her head. All of a sudden, the hours they spent in the gym came back to her. *Avoid, prevent, de-escalate, defend, fight, then run.*

Her mind clung to Danel's teachings.

She needed to get out of this. An eerie calm warmed her as her brain raced through options, pictured outcomes, considered consequences. She had to handle this.

Sunshine was sleeping alone upstairs.

It was amazing what fear for your child could do to give you focus. Drawing a deep breath, she stopped struggling and ground against his erection.

"Not so rough. You scared me." She couldn't help the tremor in her voice but hoped he was too far gone to notice. "Undo your pants while I get another pen." She glanced over her shoulder and hoped her smile seemed genuine.

Bentley eased back from her a few inches, and she reached for the pull of the drawer. When he looked down to unclasp his belt, she pulled the gun and swung. Arcing the steel with all her might, she caught him in the temple.

Confused, he staggered back.

Ronnie raised her aim and locked her stance. "Get out," she panted, her ears rushing with the thunder of dizziness taking her over. "Get out of my house right now, or I'll kill you."

He lunged, tackling her to the foyer floor. The crack of her head to the tiles brought dark spots across her vision. She grunted, fighting his strength, gripping the gun with both hands.

Bang.

Ronnie froze, the heat of blood oozing across her chest. Dizziness overwhelmed, and she blinked up at the crystals of the chandeliers. She couldn't breathe.

CHAPTER FIFTEEN

*B*rennus's treads squeaked on the rubber floor of the hospital as he tracked Storme's energy through the bustling halls. After a lifetime as an Otherworld protector and his years in the Highland armies, he knew dead. Jack was one hundy percent DOA when he checked for vitals, so what the fuck? Not that he was complaining . . . but what the fuck?

Rounding a corner into emerge, he practically crashed into Phoenix coming in from the opposite direction. The Egyptian's wings ruffled, his beast raging in his eyes. By the neon sign impression bursting off his Mark, they were far from out of the woods themselves. "You tight, my brother?"

Not even close, he signed.

Fair enough. At least Storme was handy if he went full CANDU reactor and threatened to take out the population. He fell into stride, the two of them shoulder to shoulder as heads turned and nurses decided whether to intercept the big, scary men or stare at their tight asses as they passed by.

The dark power hemorrhaging off Phoenix curdled in the pit of Brennus's stomach. Though humans weren't able to see and understand elements of the Otherworld, they would sense the threat of bodily harm pulsing their way.

That, in itself, was enough to keep them at bay.

As they passed an older woman in scrubs sitting at a desk, she looked up in alarm. He reached out with his mind and reassured her that all was well, and she should continue with her work. Storme's energy wasn't much more stable than her mate's when they found her.

Sitting beside a heart-stoppingly pale Jack, Storme's eyes still glowed a beautiful gold. Her gaze passed over him and found her husband. By the visual daggers being tossed at Phoenix, any lookie-loo onlooker from the outside wouldn't suspect that bigger than her pique at her husband was her sudden worry that he wasn't in control.

Jack's eyes cracked open, his lids half-masted and heavy. He offered up a weak smile. "Hey," he whispered.

"Hey yerself," Brennus said, taking the empty side of the bed. With his Choir-given gifts, he scanned the lad, pleased to find his essence and energy back to normal—weak, but intact. "Ye scared me back there, Jacky. What are ye doing gettin' into knife fights with no backup? We need to work on yer self-preservation skills."

Jack fidgeted with the paper-thin blanket on his chest, and Brennus gave him a minute to gather himself, switching his attention to Storme. It seemed the silent convo between her and Phoenix had ended, or at least come to a pause.

"Are ye all right, lass?"

Storme blinked up at him, shaken to the depths of the deep chocolate pools of her eyes. "How can I be? This is my fault. I never imagined Jim Logan capable of anything like this. He's a money man, a captain of industry."

"Aye, well, he isn't the first captain to kill to keep coins in the coffers." He turned to Jack. "Was it him, Jacky? Can ye identify who did this? Be verra certain because the wrath of the heavens will come down on him. Make no mistake."

Jack dipped his chin. He held up four fingers.

"There were four of them?"

He nodded.

"And Logan was the man in charge?"

He nodded again. Okay, but what Brennus didn't understand was how the young man was alive. He sensed Storme's magic and wondered if the subtle tingling of his skin was more than her presence in the cubicle.

He focused on Phoenix's mate and frowned. Exposure to the Otherworld was the biggest no-no in their lives. Their job was to police that law. If she—

"Oh, stop looking at me like that, Red," she said, waving her fingers at him. "Yes, it was me, and I'd do it again."

"Maybe we should discuss this outside," he said.

She shrugged. "No need. I already told Jack the truth."

What? If she exposed them all by telling Jack who and what they were—

She shrugged and met his gaze. "Jack knew that Cleo and I studied Wiccan practices but didn't realize true witchcraft and magic existed. Now he knows."

"Aye, it seems so. Hard to explain how a man comes back from the dead without some intervening force. He revived before ye got there though, so what did ye do?"

"I put a protection spell on him when Cleo's dealings drew undesirables into our world. When everything went to the hounds, I didn't want him hurt." She turned back to her friend and smiled. "I wouldn't let that happen."

Fuck. This put them in a bad position.

To knowingly alter the outcome of life for a human without his knowledge was one thing. To tell him she did it and used magic was another. As much as Storme considered what she did witchcraft, it was her Darkworld blood, her Shadow Caster gifts, at the source of her power.

That fell squarely into their laps.

"But all this happened before ye met Phoenix, aye?" he asked, casting her an expectant look and praying she understood the gravity of her answer. "Before yer world changed and ye found out about Cleo's history and yer own?"

She was about to answer when he raised his palm to give her a moment to think about what he asked. Her head turned to Phoenix, and he felt the flux in power as the Egyptian spoke to his wife mind-to-mind.

Her eyes widened, and she turned back to him. "Yes. *Before* I met you two and learned . . ." She glanced at Jack lying there, looking confused. "Before I learned any of it."

Brennus exhaled and nodded. Much of the human population believed that gifted people held the power to influence the outcomes of the future and perform magic and miracles. If Storme thought herself among them at the time, that should settle any conflict they'd have from above about exposure.

"Good. That's verra good, lass. And what is the blood price to pay for the deed?" All high-level spells demanded a sacrifice. It was the way the universe maintained balance.

Her gaze hardened as she brought Jack's hand to her lips and kissed her friend. "A life for a life."

Brennus nodded. "Leave that to me."

～

The sound of a gun discharging downstairs had Danel racing to the top of the railing. Below, Ronnie was pinned to the floor, Bentley on top of her, blood pooling out on the marble tile.

He threw himself over the railing, not bothering to use his wings to catch his fall. Gripping Bentley's shoulder, he flung the fucker into the far wall, denting the drywall and knocking a framed mirror from above.

A gun skittered across the floor.

An inhuman growl ripped from his throat.

Ronnie lay deathly still, her belly stained with blood. Centuries of rescue and recovery took over, the man and beast both lost to panic. "Ronnie, don't you die on me, baby."

His hands trembled as he pulled up her flannel top, running his hands over the flesh of her ribs, hips, navel. All unbroken. There was no entry wound.

Her pulse was strong, and by the time he knelt beside her and brushed her hair from her eyes, she was coming to.

Thank you, sweet Lady.

A bullet tore through his shoulder at the same time the crack of a shot fired echoed around them. He spun, his beast thoroughly engaged. Standing to his full height, he put his body between Ronnie and the plasma-smeared, Ivy League motherfucker who dared to harm her.

"What kind of a coward goes after women and shoots a man in the back?"

Bentley staggered back and squeezed off another two rounds. One ripped through his chest, the second through his palm as he went for the gun. With the full momentum of his body behind him, he plowed into the asshole and ended things on the quick.

The snap of his pencil neck had him dropping like a puppet with his strings cut. Leaning back, he howled at the ceiling, the veins in his neck strung tight.

"Danel?"

The scared voice of his mate calling his name drew him back to himself. He dropped to the floor, his knees slipping in the slick layer of blood covering the floor. "I'm here, baby. It's all right now."

"You're bleeding." She grabbed his arms, eyeing him up and down. "Oh, you're hurt."

"Nothing I won't heal from in a few hours, luv." He pulled his shirt down as she tugged on the hem. "Don't look, baby. I'm fine. Just regular, human ammunition. No red alloy. No long-term damage. As long as you're not hurt, everything is perfect. Now, give me a hug. We gotta call the police and let them take in the scene before my wounds heal."

~

Colt was out for blood—the throaty growl of his Ducati 1200cc engine bouncing off the buildings of the downtown. *Warning, good people. Steer clear. I'm in no mood.* The emotions that flooded Brennus's expression as that pretty-boy human reanimated had done him in and ripped him apart.

Affection. Relief. Hope.

He swerved to the curb and parked in the alley at the back of the RedRum. Hope. It was too much. Here he was, aching from torture, betrayed by his family, tainted by a mythical force he wanted nothing to do with, and dealing with the truth that he would never again be able to let loose for fear of releasing an ancient ice god, while his lover held hope for another man.

Someone needed to pay. Andz'gar was top of the list.

He already checked at his office, his uptown apartment, and three of his usual female fucks' homes, and found no sign of his traitorous cousin. He wasn't far.

The mighty King of Ice Demons wouldn't go into hiding. He wrapped himself in his life as an exalted leader and wouldn't do anything as intelligent as lying low.

Colt pulled the keys, took off his helmet, and stalked through the bar's smoking corral toward the back door. Gripping the handle, he stared at his gloved hands. That shit with

Zander was crazy. Since when could he project ice from his fingertips like some X-Men motherfucker?

He knew the answer and loathed it.

Avestaexa, mythical Ice God of their species.

Maybe him icing Z was a fluke. Maybe the big guy waking increased the cryokinesis of all Ice Demons. Could be. With the big kahuna stirring, they might all be juiced. Then, instead of Colt being the freak, he'd blend into the crowd.

He stepped into the back hall of the RedRum and paused to let one of J.D.'s servers pass with two Djinn males.

"Hey, cop," she said, throwing him a wink.

"Hey, Kinney." He nodded to the two males hot on her heels, about to have the time of their lives. When the three of them locked themselves into one of the private washrooms, he continued in toward the bar.

The RedRum was the kind of place where the throaty cries of females and the sweaty pump-and-grind of men enjoying a wallbanger cleared a troubled mind.

Incredibly public, yet anonymous.

A cacophony of chaos soothing his soul.

Right now, his soul needed more soothing than it ever had.

Scanning the scene, he spotted Andz'gar sitting in one of the VIP booths at the back.

Skulking in the shadows. Fitting.

The attendant gave him a nod and opened the velvet rope. As he passed, he grabbed the back of a chair, and—releasing his full force—arced the four wooden spindles through the air. The legs connected with his cousin's bodyguard and the male hit the grime of the floor like a sack of shit.

Colt spun the seat, set it over the downed man's chest, and pinned the fucker when he straddled it. "Hello, Andy."

He gave his cousin credit.

Andz'gar looked neither nervous nor surprised. He waved

off the influx of testosterone as more bodyguards rushed over. "If you expect an apology, you wasted a trip. I wasn't wrong."

Of course. Who was he to expect the egocentric, self-serving asshole, to admit he made a mistake? "Summoning a greater demon to rid yourself of an enemy, I understand, but I'm your fucking blood."

"The male about to succeed me *is* my enemy."

The guard beneath Colt's chair struggled to gain freedom. Colt tread-headed him with a solid kick, and his rocking chair fell still. Reaching across the table, he seized one of the bottles of booze and upended it.

Before he spoke, he waited for the burn of tequila to seep its way down far enough to calm the snakes writhing in his gut. "I have no interest in succeeding you."

"And that changes what?"

He took another swig. Swallow, tip, gulp. And again. And one more time. "Haven't you heard? Intention is everything."

Andz'gar chuffed. "You have never been naïve nor stupid, cousin. Once word gets out, allegiances will shift. You're of the royal line and chosen by Avestaexa to be his embodiment on earth after a thousand years of slumber."

"Bullshit. It was a blip, and I took care of it. The tale isn't gonna leak unless you open your mouth."

Andz'gar stared at the liquor swirling in his glass. "It won't be me, but it will spread. Junia saw it."

Colt cursed as nausea twisted in his gut. If Andz'gar took this to the seer and she saw his ascension . . .

"*I'm* in control of my life," he said, pleased his words sounded much more confident than he felt. "I'm a police officer and a fixer for the Otherworld. I like my life. Serve and protect. I'm good at it."

Finishing the contents of the bottle in hand, he slammed the dead soldier back to the table and moved on to one of its friends. With the next round of escape swirling in front of him, he closed his eyes and drank it all in.

He was in charge. *His* life. *His* choice.

A moment of alcohol-induced clarity sacked him in the nuts. If it were truly his choice, he'd be naked and in bed with Brennus, and his biggest worry would be how many hours of horizontal calisthenics they could squeeze in before he needed to leave for the precinct.

Instead, Brennus was holding the hand of another man.

"It's started already, I see." Andz'gar, pointed to the bottle of booze clutched in his hand. The brown glass had frosted white. "How did you do it? Attract Avestaexa's attention, I mean."

Raving wild sex. None of your fucking business. Andz'gar didn't deserve an answer. "I have no idea."

"Why did the Dark Prince protect you?"

"No idea."

Andz'gar leaned back against the cushion of the booth, his usual air of cultured shine tarnished despite his tailored Tom Ford suit. "Lie if it makes you feel better, but humble doesn't suit you."

Colt bristled, an icy chill radiating from his chest. "You think I did something to bring this on? I've been out of my mind since I felt the first crystal form in my chest. I don't want this."

"Bullshit. You play the part of the poor, disenfranchised victim, a selfless keeper of human cattle, but beneath that, you love showing me up. You never thought me a competent ruler. You never respected me or my vision."

Colt pulled the mouth of the bottle from his lips and swallowed before he choked. "That's because your vision is always about *you* and never about our people. Dismissing the Otherworld Council and siding with the Red-Metal Rebellion is a prime example. You'll put Zander and his men in a position where they have no choice but to consider us the enemy."

Andz'gar arched a dark brow. "The term 'us' no longer applies. I exiled you, remember?"

He hadn't, but now that he mentioned it, he remembered Andz'gar saying that while Brennus picked maggots from his flesh. Ice ran cold in his veins and fury burned behind his eyes.

"Telling me I'm no longer an Ice Demon doesn't mean I'm actually *not*. Changing someone's species is above your pay grade, asshole."

"Speaking of assholes, how's yours? You look worse for wear tonight. Tell me, were you the one fucked or the fucker?"

Colt closed his eyes, reining in a violent rush. "The days of homophobic bigotry are long over. Get with the times. People are free to love who they love without judgment."

Andz'gar leaned over the table, his finger pointed like a dagger at his chest. "Don't you dare use that word. Fucking a male is degrading enough. Fucking *that* male is deplorable. Do you have any idea what went on at the Dark Prince's party?"

"Don't trash him, Andy. I'm warning you."

"What's wrong, Brar'don? Can't handle hearing how—"

Colt's hearing fritzed out, and his control snapped. The rush of power that flooded his cells hit him like a surfer in the wake of a tsunami. Andz'gar's lips were still flapping as he levitated from his chair. Rising into the air, he gripped his fingers into fists, his entire body shaking with cold fury.

"Shut your mouth," he said, his voice booming from all angles. "Do *not* speak Brennus of Eire. Not. Another. Word."

Unimaginable pulses of power built within. It chilled his muscles and bones, and burned under his skin. He was fire and ice. He was past and present. He vaguely heard Andz'gar cry out, noticed the bastard's face contort in pain, felt the bite of frost on his own face.

Andz'gar lilted to the side, his body iced over. In a small part of his cranium, Colt knew he should be afraid, but was lost to something greater than himself.

Why had he feared this?

He was the embodiment of Ice Demon ancestry. He was the keeper of their journey from Heaven to Hell to Earth. He was himself, yet more.

He was a god.

CHAPTER SIXTEEN

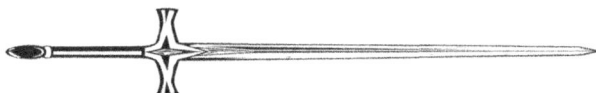

*B*rennus released the shoulders of Jim Logan, and his lifeless body dropped to the carpeted floor with the others. "One blood sacrifice paid in full. Imagine the confusion in the morgue tonight. How do four healthy men have a cataclysmic cardiac rupture at the same time? No drugs. No signs of trauma. It's one medical mystery they'll never quite figure out."

He held up his fist and Phoenix met it with a bump. The rigid fury of Storme being threatened and her assistant targeted was addressed with equal force as Jack's throat being slashed.

With justice served, his brother's beast eased a great deal.

Brennus stepped over the bodies, which other than them no longer having a pulse, remained fully intact. "Yer gettin' wicked talented, Egyptian. Glad yer on our side."

Phoenix finished going through Logan's briefcase files, while he made one final sweep of the hotel room before heading over to the open window.

The other investors know Storme and my mother practice witchcraft. This should convince them that coming after her in the future is detrimental to their health.

Brennus was about to dematerialize back to the ranch to call it a night when his comm activated in his ear. "We've got an all-call at the Rum, boys," Tanek said, his voice weird. "Drop what you're doing and get over there. Zander's on scene."

Reaching out with his mind, Brennus turned off the lights and made sure the door was locked. "On our way. Have we got anyone at the Royal York?"

"One sec." There was a quiet tapping of keys, and then Tanek came back online. "A Darkworld male on maintenance and a Lightworld female on the front desk."

"Send the maintenance man to Logan's room to find the bodies. I don't want to scar an innocent human lass working housekeeping."

"Will do. Get to the Rum, Celt. ASAP."

"Aye, heading there now." With a nod to Phoenix, the two of them dematerialized from the shadows of the Royal York Hotel over to the Darkworld bar.

Zander's hedonist club, O-Zone, offered members of the Otherworld a safe zone, where everyone was welcome to come and mingle—the RedRum was Darkworld only. This place was less about the music and mingle and more about sex, drugs, and duplicitous dealings.

Which was exactly why it rocked.

Darkworlders needed a place of their own, someplace to focus their least desirable behaviors without judgment or even opinions weighing in. That was the RedRum.

Taking form in the shadows of the alley around back, the first thing Brennus noticed was the electric blue Ducati parked at the curb. Shit. That got his ticker pumping. Jogging around to the smoker's area, he met Zander blocking the entrance.

As warriors bred by the Archangels to serve, they were all toned muscle on large frames and held themselves with a great deal of aggression, but Zander topped that level of aggression over all of them—even before he transitioned into a full Dark Angel. The fact that the Sumerian had his feet planted and was playing the part of an offensive lineman blocking the door sent a cold shaft through the Celt's junk.

"Tell me," Brennus snapped.

"Any idea how Colt Creed grew a foot and turned the Rum into a snow globe scene from *The Day After Tomorrow?*

Blood rushed from Brennus's head and he grabbed the rail of the wooden corral fence to brace himself. "Is he all right?"

"Hard to know what all right looks like in this scenario, Celt. The guy is frosted over like he spent a year in a walk-in freezer and needs time to thaw. What in all that's unholy are we dealing with?"

"It's complicated," Brennus said, his mind and heart at war over which one got to start convulsing first.

"Complicated. Yeah, that's what I hear, but that shit ain't helping. We need deets, my brother, right-fucking-now. What's going on?"

Brennus cursed and wiped a hand over his face, trying to sort through the scrambled mess of his brain. "There's this ancient ice god, Avestaexa, who lives within the veins of the royal line of Ice Demons. He's been dormant for a thousand years, but stirred inside Colt a few months ago."

Zander recoiled. "And you *knew* this?"

He met the worried gazes of his warrior brothers gathered and shook his head. "I had no idea why he went AWOL. He kicked me to the curb, and I was in the dark, same as you."

"What changed?"

"Shayton showed me a book of lore while the cop was recovering. Colt thought since the entity only stirred and hadn't woken completely, that he could hold the thing at bay if he stayed tight and kept things simple."

Zander spun his massive silver skull ring over his thumb and frowned. "Well, that bit him in the ass. He popsicled his cousin, and is now holding Darkworlder court in there, catching up on the state of the union."

"How many hostages?"

Zander shrugged. "At this time of night, my guess would be close to two dozen."

"We need eyes on the inside," Kyrian said.

"So," Seth asked, "who are we dealing with in there? Is it the cop, the ancient Have-a-steaks-a guy, or a combo platter of the two males?"

Brennus tried to recall what he'd read. "I dinnae ken. Colt made it sound like waking the guy meant the end for him."

That hit all of them the same way. Colt was more than a fellow warrior fighting the fight. He was a friend.

"Well, if our boy is still in there somewhere," Kyrian said, "we gotta bring him to the foreground long enough to get a read on things."

Zander exhaled, his long brown hair swishing and brushing his arms as he shook his head. "He's contained at the moment, but if this ice god asshole decides to stretch his legs and hit the town, we're fucked."

Hark scrubbed a hand over his bald, black head. "What about the glamor spell Storme cast to hide Phoenix's battle with Asmodeus? Something like that could help."

Zander nodded. "Good idea. Egyptian, get her down here."

Phoenix raised his hands with a shit-ton of hells-no in his scowl when Zander cut him off.

"Set her up"—he glanced around and pointed to the roof of a building a good distance up the street—"over there. Stay with her and use your power to amplify her spell."

Kyrian shifted his feet, looking antsy. "You sure bringing Storme into this is a good idea, *Adelphos*?"

"I have to believe Colt's in there somewhere. If he is, he won't harm her. Masking Otherworld chaos shouldn't set off any alarm bells and put him on the defensive. If I'm wrong," he said, meeting Phoenix's gaze, "if he so much as glances in your direction, fly her out."

The two of them stood staring at one another for a long moment before Phoenix dematerialized to fetch his wife.

"Maybe he won't even come out to play," Seth offered.

"If it were you and you'd been asleep for a millennium, wouldn't you want to take a look around at the world?"

The warrior nodded. "Yeah, we're fucked. Should we call down the assholes in white?"

The wave of cursing proved that everyone hated that idea with equal measure.

"What about the dragons?" Hark asked.

Zander cursed. "Dragons against an ancient ice god in the heart of Toronto? That's a bad Godzilla movie waiting to happen."

Seth flexed his wings, his mighty brawn tight with tension. "There is no bad Godzilla movie, but I get your point. Anyone else miss the good ole days of guns and knives. When our enemy came at us with physical force, and we got beat up and sweaty, taking out the trash?"

"Instead, we get a god planning a spree of evil," Bo said.

"Ohmygod, it's a spreevil," Seth added.

For fuck's sake. Brennus tipped his head back and saw nothing of the night sky above. A screamer of a headache pounded in his skull. Maybe it was a tumor about to rupture and put him out of his misery. "Let me go see what I can find out. If Colt's in there anywhere, he'll listen to me."

Zander swept his hand toward the entrance and shifted to let him pass. "Have at it, my brother. You're our best shot."

Taking that as his cue, Brennus headed inside.

Poor Colt. He hadn't wanted this. He didn't deserve this. He'd been willing to sacrifice his own life's happiness not to become everything he'd worked to fight against.

Walking up the hallway, his labored breath came out in misty white clouds. The powerful surge of energy ahead woke his gift and had his heartbeat thundering in his ears.

The door to one of the private washrooms opened on his left, and he froze. He halted the trio emerging, and pressed a finger to his lips. Pointing at the back door, he signaled for them to take their leave. When one of the guys made like he might argue, Brennus cut that shit off with a look and gestured to the exit once more.

The female seemed to understand, and led the retreat.

Once the door closed, he eased up the hall, listening to the convo being laid out in the main bar. Ah, the god was thirsty and anxious to get his buzz on.

Pausing in the shadowed entryway, his brain stalled out. What was he seeing? A place he knew like the back of his hand was frosted, wall-to-wall, the floors covered with a thin layer of ice, long spears of icicles hanging from lighting fixtures and the corners of tables.

To his right, JD and one of his bartenders upended bottles of booze and worked the blender like their asses were on fire. To his left, three booths and two tables of Darkworlders looked like they might dirty their breeks, if they hadn't already. And straight ahead, against the far wall, was an unholy version of Colt Creed, sitting atop a raised dais of ice shaped into a throne.

"Brennus of Eire," Colt said in a voice that held none of the familiar warmth of his lover. He gestured to the seat set in front of him and flicked his hand at the Djinn sitting there to vacate. "Join me."

As he raised his palms and inched his way forward, his comm activated in his ear with a gentle beep. "We're right with you, Celt," Tanek said. "We've got full audio and visual."

It didn't escape him that he could be dead in a split-second if Avestaexa wished it so. He glanced to the floor by Colt's feet. Yep, Andz'gar, Ice Demon King was one traitorous popsicle.

"I see ye got yer justice, cop. Ye deserved that, at least." He lowered himself onto the chair, set his hands on the leather of his thighs, and braced his heart. After a deep breath, he lifted his chin and met the gaze of his possessed lover.

The male assessing him was every bit the same man he had ever been—and at the same time, not. The same short blond-brown hair framed his strong, square jaw. The same lithe, athletic frame highlighted his physical beauty.

Not his eyes. Those were wrong.

Colt's stunning cerulean blue had been replaced by an eerie gold. Not the warm, whiskey gold of Danel and Ringo, but a solid surface of glimmering metallic ore.

"Are ye in there, cop?" he said, his voice choked. The male's eyes remained devoid of Colt's fire, but he thought he saw a flicker of recognition. Wishful thinking? "If ye are, know that I'm here fer ye . . . we all are."

The male looked off to where a couple was huddled in the corner of the room. "He wishes you gone."

That connected like a sucker punch to the sack.

Brennus swallowed. "I agreed to keep my distance fer safety's sake, but now that yer here anyway, all bets are off. I'll not be sent away again."

"That displeases him. Queer. Even with his consciousness suppressed, my host holds more fear for you confronting me than for his own well-being."

Brennus exhaled. "That doesna surprise me. Colt is solid like that. He's a good male. Loyal, strong, and the most stubborn soul I ever crossed dicks with."

The lazy smirk that lifted the corner of his mouth was all Colt. He was sure of it.

"He regards you as his general. Why?"

Brennus tapped his gold ring and ran the woven braid of his hair through his fingers. "Long ago, in another land and lifetime, I led armies in some of the major wars in history. My *nom de guerre* was the General."

He frowned, looking perplexed. "That is not his meaning,

though. He uses it as a term of endearment. You are *his* general. He regards you with a depth of affection. He draws strength from you. He dreams of a future with you, though he wants not for you to know."

Brennus's breath escaped his lungs as his beast surged forward. Whether he said the words or not, he'd known. Colt's protective nature was more than fear of him getting caught up in the danger of the prophecy.

Sending him away didn't mask anything. Brennus's gift from the Choir was reading Otherworld mojo.

Colt's feelings had a very definite signature.

"I love you too, cop," he said, searching the male's body language and expression for any sign of Colt. "Ye slipped under my radar, when I wasnae lookin', and claimed a place in my cold, dark heart I didnae ken was there. That's why ye gotta stay strong. Dinnae let yerself be consumed by this."

The ice god straightened in his seat and held up his palm. A tall, pink drink with two umbrellas appeared in his hand, and he sipped on the bendy-straw. "You speak as if he and I are separate, General. The moment I woke, we—god and mortal male—began merging to become one."

The idea that Colt was to be absorbed into a maniacal ice god made Brennus sick. Was there any way to stop this?

If there was, he had no clue what it was.

CHAPTER SEVENTEEN

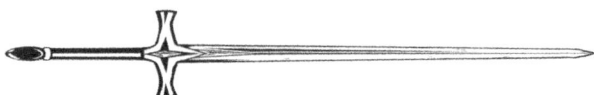

*D*anel set the suitcases down in the foyer and closed the door behind them. It was good to be home. Home. He never thought that word would hold any meaning for him beyond the empty promises of what others had, and he didn't. He took Sunshine from Ronnie's arms and kissed his wife on the cheek. "Pass me the carrier and then take a load off in the kitchen for a bit. I'll put sweetness and the furball to bed and come make you that peppermint tea you like."

Ronnie practically swayed on her feet. "Sounds perfect."

This past week took a lot out of her, but being back at the ranch with Austin and the wives would give her the support system to find her footing again.

Climbing the stairs, he hugged Sunshine close to his chest and brushed his lips over her blonde curls.

How had he earned the right to be so happy?

He set Rascal's cat carrier on the carpet inside Sunshine's bedroom door and took his baby girl over to her bed. After fixing her blankies and tucking her in, he freed the furball and set him on the end of the bed.

"You be good, Rascal. You're a guest in this house, and I'm

not above dropping you off at the shelter if you scratch her again or cause any trouble." Not that he would.

Sunshine had quickly taken the reins of his beast and wrapped them in her tiny hands. He could do nothing other than give her everything she wanted. Which Ronnie said had to stop.

Whatevs.

Straightening, he went into the bathroom to turn on the Supernatural nightlight and check that Tanek set up a litterbox and food station for the kitten. Yep, they were all set and . . . he eyed the new door on the opposite wall and smiled.

Opening the thing up, he found his and Ronnie's bathroom next door. Sweet. Adjoining rooms.

Could things get any better?

Leaving things open and accessible to the now adjoining suites, he set a glass of water on the bedside table and kissed his girlie goodnight. "May Lady Divinity keep you safe and guide you all your days, sweet Sunshine."

He closed her door and headed back to his wife, but first, he passed the stairs and went to the other end of the second floor to check in with—holy shit.

Ringo sat ramrod stiff at his desk, his eyes rolled back in his head, his drawing pen moving in a blur over an art pad he wasn't even glancing at.

Was it some kind of a trance? A premonition?

The kid's precog abilities had all of them scratching their heads in wonder. If he was this strong before his fifteenth birthday, what would happen when he transitioned in a few weeks . . . and again when he found his mate?

Not wanting to disturb his little brother, he took out his phone and started recording. Easing silently over the carpet, he closed in on what he was working on.

Ringo paid him no attention.

Danel doubted the kid was aware of anything within his

surroundings. The soft scratch of felt nib to paper continued, the image unfolding with preternatural divining.

He stepped behind him and got a good look at the drawing. What the hell did it mean?

After making sure he captured the mysterious masterpiece on his phone, he backed out and beat feet downstairs. Jogging down the corridor, he found Ronnie sitting at the table, chatting with Austin.

"Hey, cowgirl." Leaning in to kiss her cheek, he noticed the tea and squares set out on the table. "Looks like you beat me at taking care of my girl. Is there anything I can get you two ladies?"

Austin smiled, the circles under her hazel eyes making her look tired. "We're fine here, catching up on things. I'm sorry to say, I think you're needed elsewhere. Something's gone wrong with Colt."

He wondered if it was the same shit with Asmodeus or a different pile of shit. "So, it's a 'welcome home, get back to work' sorta deal?"

Austin nodded. "Sorry to be the bearer of bad news."

Danel grabbed a square and met Ronnie's gaze. "Is that okay with you, baby? There's shit hitting, but I can bail if you need me, or stick to back-up from the war room."

Ronnie set her mug on the coaster and smiled up at him. "Off you go, warrior. Back to normal is exactly what I need. Go play with your friends."

Danel loved that she could make light of what they did. He gauged her sincerity, and when he was sure she was good with him leaving, he ducked down and pressed his lips against her mouth. "Love you."

"Love you more."

He grabbed two more squares for the road and shook his head. "Impossible."

With purpose in his stride, he went down to the war room

and found Tanek working the bank of monitors and the comm system. Danel stared at the indoor winter wonderland showing on the main screen and noted the notation in the bottom right. "Where the fuck is Brennus and—what the—is that Colt?"

Tanek rose from his chair and met him chest to chest. "Glad to have you home, Persian. Sorry I couldn't be there with the rest of them for you yesterday."

Danel shook off the regret and patted the guy's back before breaking free. "You've always been there for me, T. Don't give it another thought. What's going on?"

They got back to business, and Tanek gave him the low-down on Colt unlocking an ancient ice god. "There's a fuck-ton of weirdness in air right now, D. Not sure what's going on with the world."

"Speaking of weirdness—this happened." He pulled out his phone and called up the video of Ringo upstairs. "Have you ever seen him do that?"

Tanek watched the replay of their prophetic artist in a sight-less trance and frowned. After an encore viewing, he scratched his head. "That's fucking freaky."

"Adds to the weirdness factor, right?"

Tanek checked the screens and then came back to him. "What is that drawing telling us?"

Danel took another look at the image and paused it on the drawing pad. Storme and the old lady from Bo's wedding were head-to-head, looking grim and focused. "It's hard to say, but I think I better get down to the Rum and show it to Z. Knowing Ringo, it's gonna tie in somehow."

Tanek nodded. "Okay, get down there. I'll let him know you're on your way."

Danel turned for the door. "I'll gear up, take another shot of the kid's progress, and be there in five."

Making small talk with the ice god assimilating your lover isn't as easy as you'd think. Staring at a bizarre eight-foot version of Colt, Brennus wanted to scream, to stab the guy, to shake him until he vacated Colt's body and left them alone. Avestaexa was awake and captaining Colt's ship. And from what Colt said, it wouldn't be long before the guy started enslaving humanity.

Talk about Otherworld exposure.

"How long," he asked, his voice cracking, "until the two of you are fully integrated?"

Avestaexa sipped the last of his fruity concoction and used his powers to call for another from the bar. "He is a complex male. Historically, my hosts were rather one-dimensional. Evil daemons driven to get what Hell and the realms owes them. I assimilate those types quickly. Your male is different. He holds himself to a standard. His ambitions aren't self-serving."

"Yet still ye want to take him over," Brennus said, a bite in his tone. He gripped the tops of his knees, wanting to gut the bastard but unable to do anything without harming Colt.

"Have ye ever thought there are things to learn from the males ye possess, that there's more to life than conquering those less powerful than yerself?"

Brennus watched the male's aura as he spoke, the heavy strands of gold and black strangling and consuming the smoky blue-gray of Colt's mojo. He wanted to cry.

Talking wasn't getting him anywhere. He needed to bring Colt forward. Without thought, Brennus launched forward and gripped the god's face, pulling his mouth to his.

With all the energy he had, he called to Colt, swept those lips he loved to taste, bent the male back in his ice throne until he nearly broke him in half.

Come on, cop. Where's the fire. I know yer in there.

His heart ached, pounding behind his ribs as he willed his lover forward. His tongue slipped through the seam of his lips and speared into his mouth. Firm fingers tightened at his nape and gripped him by the hair.

Afraid Avestaexa would pull him back, Brennus bit his lip and laved the blood over both their tongues. The male groaned, gripping at the waistband of his leathers.

Brennus's eyes flew wide, and he met the cerulean gaze he longed for. "There ye are, cop. Thank fuck."

If a huge PDA was his only chance to save him, he'd gladly place himself on the alter for consumption. Besides, after Shayton's party, he didn't have an ounce of modesty left.

～

Colt surged forward, the fog he'd been drowning beneath suddenly giving way to powerful clarity. And what was the first thing he saw as he bobbed to the surface? The stunning gaze of his warrior. Grappling onto the lifeline Brennus offered, Colt let his worry and reluctance go. If they only had this one last moment, he wanted it to be everything they'd never had.

He wished he had a proper bed to lay him on.

The moment the thought occurred to him, they were naked and laid out on his massive mattress in his home. If he wasn't losing his mind, he might've stopped to wonder about that.

But really, who the fuck cared?

He cupped the warrior's heavy, hard sex. "I love you, B. I need you to know that."

They kissed with a shared desperation, terrified that at any moment, he'd lose his hold and be lost to the ice god who'd obligingly taken a back seat for the moment.

On a hard yank, Brennus rolled over him, spreading his thighs and shifting over him until their hard cocks rubbed together between them.

They both cursed, but not in a bad way.

Nothing about the two of them together skin-on-skin, the

friction of their erections rubbing, the frenzy of the wet heat of their mouths consuming one another, could ever be bad.

Dizzy from the blood pounding through his body, Colt tried to breathe. If this was his last moment on earth, he could die a happy man. There was too much hunger to make sense of whose hands were where and how so much pleasure could be rushing at him from every angle.

"Yes. Fuck, yes." Colt came with a rough shout, his balls clenching tight, slick, hot cum drenching their abdomens.

With a quick shift, Brennus broke away from his mouth, and swiped down his abs with a rough hand, gathering the mess they made. The world went topsy-turvy, and Colt thought for a moment he lost his hold on the ice god.

Then his face got mashed into his pillow. No, the world was fine. Brennus had flipped him onto his belly.

Colt got with the program fast and rose to his knees. All that spent cream the Celt gathered off their flesh got put to good use, and a moment later, Brennus pressed up behind. . .

"May I take the honors?"

"Please," he gasped, desperation in his voice.

This was the two of them, raw and honest.

Gasoline and flamethrower. Hunger and feast.

Brennus thrust inside with a lightning-fast strike and Colt nearly came again right then. Planting his palms on the mattress he braced himself for the powerful, punishing rhythm he knew was coming.

The squelch of his bed moving over the floor echoed loud and he was sure could be heard down the block. He didn't fucking care. This burn, the pressure, and the pleasure was all that mattered. They were not stopping this time.

No withdrawals. No miscommunications.

This was their one chance to devour one another, and he wanted every bit of power Brennus held in his mighty warrior body, every thrust and retreat, every grunt and groan.

Brennus tightened one hand on his hip and the other in his hair. Colt's breath escaped as his head snapped back, and the Celt used the newfound leverage to keep pumping, pumping, pumping...

Adjusting his hips, Colt widened his stance so his warrior could get inside him as hard and deep as possible. The sensation had him gasping for breath, panting for more, his balls burning with the need to explode again.

"Yer mine, cop," he growled, behind him. "I'm laying my claim. Got it?"

He punctuated his point by reaching around his hips and gripping his cock. The connection was too much, too hot. Colt let off a shout, and Brennus came right along with him. They orgasmed together, their throaty grunts all male, all ecstasy.

Brennus collapsed over his back and Colt chuckled at the crushing weight. The guy was spent, his breath escaping in harsh bursts.

Eventually, Colt's heart slowed and his muscles stopped burning. Rolling to the side, Brennus gathered him in his arms. Still joined, he spooned him, his lips brushing against the sweaty flesh of his neck.

"Consider yerself mate, Colt," he whispered against his ear. "I'll not let anyone take ye from me."

Brennus nipped his ear, a slick hand drifting lazily up his navel to his pecs. The growl that filled the room thickened his cock as if his body were enthralled. "Now that we've fucked hard to take the edge off, we're gonna slow things down and take our time."

Colt looked down at the arms holding him and blinked back the sting of tears. Brennus's Mark glowed silver. It was so fucking beautiful Colt could hardly breathe. His Watcher had claimed him.

Him. A filthy demon who no one had ever cared for.

"I love you, B." He arched against the languid push and pull of the Celt behind him and the warrior hissed. "And I'm so fucking scared."

Brennus wrapped his arms tighter. "Whatever happens, cop. We'll figure it out."

The drugging fog from before crept in from the corners of his mind and Colt's heart raced. He gripped Brennus's arm, his tears taking hold. "Fuck, he's taking over again. I don't want to go. I don't want to lose this."

And then, the fog washed over him once again.

CHAPTER EIGHTEEN

*Z*ander didn't know what happened. One minute, they were waiting outside the Rum for Brennus to give them a foothold on what they were dealing with, and then the next, Tanek came over the comm, saying Brennus had left the building. "What do you mean, gone?" he asked, signaling for Seth and Hark to check it out.

"Just that," Tanek said in his ear. "Talking wasn't getting him anywhere, so he tried another tack and then *poof,* the visual was lost, and the audio got real interesting, real fast."

"What kind of interesting?"

"Um, the kind when you close the office door and leave the couple to enjoy themselves."

Zander met the wide-eyed confusion of Kyrian and the others. "His other tack was to seduce the evil ice god?"

"I think his goal was to draw Colt forward. Seemed to be working too, from what I gathered."

Hark and Seth came trotting out of the bar, and Seth took the lead. "T's right. He's gone."

Kyrian frowned. "And what happens when this seduction

plan goes bad? We have no idea where they are or how to back him up."

"Where who is?" Danel said, rounding the corner of the smoker's corral and jogging up to meet them.

"Welcome home, Persian." Zander clasped his brother's hand and caught him up. "So, here we stand, no idea where they are and no idea how to fix it once we do."

"I might have a lead on that," Danel said. He tapped his comm and looked up the street. "Phoenix, can you bring your better half down here, please. Ringo sees her involved in the next part of this."

Then, he pulled out his phone and called up a video of their youngest brother.

"That's a fucking freak show," Zander said, watching the kid's hand whizzing over the drawing pad with his eyes rolled back, like some kind of possessed zombie.

"It was worse standing two feet away, let me tell you."

The others crowded in, and the video got passed around. Once Phoenix and Storme arrived, they got their turn. "Check out the drawing," Danel said, pointing at the phone. "That's you and the Djinn elder from Bo's wedding. What do you think the two of you are doing?"

"We're saving the world," the old woman said, hobbling along the sidewalk to join them. Dressed, as usual, in a richly colorful silk kimono, the woman carried herself like a queen despite her years.

"Neima," Bo said, rushing to greet the ancient seer of the Djinn people. He greeted his brother-in-law, Gheil, with a clasped hand, and then bent at the waist and brought the old woman's knotted knuckles to his lips. "I assume you've seen something very important. Why else would a female of your stature come to a place like this."

She patted his hand and winked. "In my day, I certainly wasn't as refined as I am now. You might be shocked, warrior."

As Bo chuckled, Neima extended her reach around him and toward Storme. "Come, child. We have much to do and no time to waste."

~

The moment Colt was gone, Brennus pulled back and rolled off the bed. His heart shattered. There was no logical reason to believe that him arousing Colt would hold him as the dominant power over a god, but part of him had hoped.

"Don't look so sad, General. If it makes you feel better, the sex we shared filled your male with a sense of belonging and acceptance he longed for all his life."

Was that supposed to make him feel better?

"Why is your skin aglow like that?"

Brennus wanted to tell Avestaexa to shove his curiosity up his ass, but what good would that serve? "I am Nephilim—half-human and half-archangel. When my kind bond with another, and that bond is threatened, our most violent impulses are triggered, and our Marks glow."

"It is quite beautiful. *You* are quite beautiful."

Brennus couldn't stand having those gold, pupilless eyes staring at him, naked, sweaty, and spent. He stormed into Colt's bathroom and cleaned up. After washing and wrapping a towel around his male parts, he tucked the end of the black terry against his hip and returned to the bedroom.

"Why does my appreciation of your physique spark your anger. A moment ago, we were joined in body and the throes of passion."

"That was Colt, not you."

He tilted his head, his lazy smirk far too much like the male he possessed. "I felt the pleasure of your passion. I was present and aware, as he is now while I speak with you. There is no him or me. We are one."

Brennus didn't know what to say or think about that. When he'd been with Colt, he'd been *with* Colt. That another male had watched or felt or shared in that made him want to kill someone. "That was for us, not you."

"Why?"

"Because no one invites a maniacal ice god into their love. Yer an unwelcome intruder."

Leaning his naked ass on the dresser, Avestaexa frowned and crossed his ankles. It was a position he'd seen Colt take a hundred times over the years. He hated how much this male mimicked his host. "I am a god. Why would you choose him over me? I can give you anything. There are no bounds to my powers."

Now it was Brennus's turn to frown. "Save the 'I'm all-powerful' bullshit for someone else, frosty. Yer not the first god I've met, and unless ye kill me tonight, I doubt you'll be the last. There are always boundaries and limitations to powers. Yin and Yang. Good and evil. Light and Dark."

"Everything is weighted in the balance, that is true."

Brennus spotted his clothes on the floor and rounded the bed to get dressed. Once he was put back together, he sank onto the bed. He was tired and sad and scared and, for the life of him, he had no idea what to do next. He didn't want to leave Colt, but he didn't know how to help him.

"I find . . ." he said, looking puzzled. "Strangely, I do not wish you gone. I enjoy conversing with you."

"Why?" Brennus said, throwing his hands in the air. "What about any of this are ye enjoying?"

Avestaexa regarded him and pondered the question. "You aren't afraid of me. You don't cower or have any interest in gaining my favor. You simply are."

Brennus raked his fingers through his hair and exhaled. "I've lived millennia, ye ken. I've loved. I've killed. I've seen the best of people and the worst. I dinnae fear for myself any longer.

Now, I fear for those I love. If ye want me dead, I'll be dead. It's as simple as that."

The male stood and stepped closer, reaching as if he wanted to touch him but held back. "I do not wish you dead, Brennus of Eire. I wish more of your company. I find you intriguing. I find you physically attractive. My host loves you, and I find I am quite captivated as well. After lying in a dormant sleep for ages, I find our interaction stimulating."

Brennus heard the first hint of hope in the male's words. Was this his answer? Was he willing to flirt with the bastard who held his mate prisoner?

"Ye said the male's ye've possessed in the past were always dark, selfish, driven males, and that's the path ye took in their lives. What if, instead of taking control of others, and stealing lives, and living in isolation, ye tried rising to a new challenge and living *with* us instead of lording yerself over us?"

He straightened, lifting his chin. "Explain."

Brennus searched for the words, terrified to get this wrong. "Ye have possession of Colt, but he's not gone. If ye merge with yer hosts, ye know he protects people, he doesna kill them without cause. He helps innocents thrive in this realm, and he doesna demand adoration or subservience in return. He's a male of worth. Have ye ever tried letting yer host take the lead? Ye might learn a thing or two. The realms have changed a great deal over the millennia."

Avestaexa seemed to consider it.

Brennus's beast paced within. The two auras were almost completely merged, and he feared the two were now one.

"What do ye say? Will ye work with me on this? With the strength of yer power and the life Colt has in place, ye have the potential to do great things." Brennus swallowed, sending up a prayer that what he proposed held interest.

If he were an ancient ice god, he would get bored if all he did was kill and enslave people.

Avestaexa leaned down until their lips hovered inches apart. "You. Are. Adorable. General." A sly grin broke the tension in his expression, and he chuckled. "Why would I—an omniscient being of power—take second position?"

"What about the isolation? Wouldn't ye like to work with yer host for once—have a partner in this life?"

His grin became a full-blown smile. "Oh, but I do have a partner. Brennus of Eire, you shall stay by my side and serve as my confidant and advisor."

∼

Storme considered herself a high-level witch but listening to Neima explain what they needed to do, she was well over her depths. Even with Phoenix's help, she didn't see how they would be able to bind the will of a god.

She glanced over to her husband, waiting with his brothers at the bar, while she and Neima worked through the details and possible consequences of the spell. For every spell, there was a price to pay and for one this integral and demanding, she was afraid to imagine the cost.

She focused on the ingredients simmering in the iron skillet they were using as a caldron. The platinum ring they'd conjured had to be perfectly enchanted.

Thanks to J.D., they had all the tools and ingredients needed to fabricate the thing. Thanks to Ringo's drawing, they had a detailed diagram of Brennus's ring to follow.

"You complete the spell, child." Neima sank into the booth across from her and waved Phoenix over. "Direct the power needed to infuse the invocation until it takes hold and the ring glows silver. Whatever happens, you must not break the flow of power, or it will fail. I've seen every outcome, and this must succeed or the world will suffer."

Phoenix joined them, and she was thankful, yet again, that

he was the bomb when it came to all things dangerous and life-altering. His mother, Cleo, lacked in many areas, but she was a powerful witch, and Storme doubted anyone else could harness her magic the way Phoenix could.

"Watcher," Neima said, holding out her hand. "Loan me your dagger for a moment."

Not a good idea, he signed, and she translated for him.

Gheil rushed over, the Master of Djinn understandably concerned. A Watcher's Crystalline dagger had a hollow shaft, its core infused with Seraph blood. They were the ultimate weapons and cut down Darkworlders without any chance of defense. "You don't need his weapon, Neima. There's no way I will permit you to hurt yourself."

Neima arched a brow and frowned. "Mind your elder, boys. Pass me the dagger, lickety quick. This spell calls for a blood sacrifice, and my Djinn powers of mind manipulation will strengthen the ring's effectiveness."

"Then I'll do it," Gheil said, thrusting his hand toward Phoenix.

"No," Neima said, shaking her head. "I have seen the outcomes. It must be me. This ice god must not rise to reign again. It ends with us."

Phoenix looked to his commander, who, after a moment of consideration, gave him the go-ahead nod. Reluctantly, he unsheathed his blade and handed it over.

"Be very careful, milady," Zander said, holding out his hands as if he wanted to snatch the blade out of her grasp. "The dagger is wicked sharp and will cut deeper and more easily than you expect."

Neima waved away his concern, wrapped her gnarled fingers around the razor edge of the blade, and drew the dagger free. A hiss fell from her lips at the same time blood rushed from her clenched palm. She held her fist over the caldron, and her blood sizzled with the other ingredients.

After a moment, she looked up at them with utter peace in her faded green eyes. "Don't look so worried, gentlemen. What is done is done. The spell is cast and will not be broken."

Zander ripped a clean bar towel into strips and wrapped Neima's hand. "You honor us with your help."

Neima batted her eyes up at the Sumerian and chuckled. "The ring won't do us much good if we don't know where the ice god is. Find him, warrior. The next stage will be up to you and your men."

Zander kissed her bound hand and went back to the bar.

Storme refocused on the sizzling skillet and the ring glowing red in the center.

"Now then, quiet one," she said, smiling up at Phoenix. "This next bit falls on your broad shoulders. Read the invocation exactly as we prepared it—in your head is fine—and focus on the ring. Only the ring. No matter what happens, you must not stop until it glows a swirling silver with Djinn magic."

Storme smiled at her husband. They both knew what that looked like. They saw that beautiful swirling silver every day in baby Zane's eyes. "Okay, let's do this."

Phoenix shifted the notebook with the spell before him and studied the words. A moment later, she felt his power build. As it rose in strength, Storme funneled the magic into the ring, pressing her fingers on the black, velvet choker that bound the two of them, in an effort to heighten their connection.

"That's right," Neima said. "Don't stop, children."

Storme watched as the ring absorbed the herbs and ingredients smoking and sizzling on the surface of the skillet. She struggled to funnel the influx of Phoenix's power and the intention of the spell. His magic was so far beyond anything she'd ever trained with, or even understood.

She looked over at him for a split-second to gauge his control. His eyes were white, his ebony wings wide, and his Mark glowing green. Gritting her teeth, she worked as a conduit for his energy. It arced in her cells, burned her finger-tips, and thrummed in her veins.

As things built, the vibrations of the spell had the table jiggling in place. The subtle bump grew to a rumble and threat-ened to jostle their setup beneath Phoenix's ministrations. She focused on the energy. The shift in essence confused her at first, the new energy signature unfamiliar. The ring pulsed, the glowing red of molten metal becoming less orange.

"It's working," she said, watching as gray tones overtook the vibrance. The rumble of the table's vibration picked up, and she gripped the edge of the table, trying to hold things down.

"On it," Seth said, climbing over the back of the neighboring booth to stand on their table. His near three-hundred pounds pressed the wooden surface to the floor once more.

Storme glanced up to smile at her brother-in-law, and saw his attention firmly locked on Neima. She gasped when she saw the Djinn seer. Hunched and withering, the woman looked like she'd aged twenty years in three minutes.

"Don't stop," Neima said, pointing a curled finger. "This is the only way humanity survives. I've seen it."

Storme stared at the ring, the metal no longer red, but a dull gray. Maybe that was enough. Maybe they didn't need every-thing Neima was willing to sacrifice.

"Stop this," Gheil said, realizing what Neima had done.

"Trust me, children," Neima said, her voice weak as she slumped into the Djinn Master's arms. "My life, so millions may live? A fair trade, I say."

Storme blinked past tears, feeling the strength of the Djinn essence fading through her as the ring gained luster. The cost was high. She should have thought more about that, about why Neima wanted to be the one to supply the blood.

"I'm so sorry," she said, her throat tight.

Neima rested her hand over her wrist. "I am at peace."

As the last of Neima's energy exited the funnel of power, the ring glowed a beautiful swirling silver. Storme stared at the thing they'd created, the thing that took the life of another.

Hot tears ran down her cheeks.

It was only then that Phoenix's beast became aware of his surroundings. Her sorrow brought his full attention, and she tilted her head toward Neima's body. Entranced as he was, he'd missed the sacrifice of the old Djinn seer.

Did I do that?

She took his hand. "No. It was her intention when she scored her hand and committed to the blood sacrifice."

Reaching for the ring, she cooled it off with a quick incantation and handed it to Zander. "Get this to Brennus and end this. Let Neima's death be worth something."

~

Bo entered the loft with Gheil at his side and no idea how to tell Layne what happened. His mate loved that old woman. She'd been a surrogate grandmother to her after her parents were killed. She was the one who guided her, and pushed her when she needed it. And she was dead.

"Yay, you're home," she said, straightening from the old war table, her research and papers her constant preoccupation. "I think I'm close. I've tracked the Rugaru down to two possible places, both on the same block."

When she looked up, she saw her brother and frowned. "Gheil? Why are you here?"

"We have bad news, luv," Bo said, extending a hand for her to join him.

Her emerald eyes jumped from him to her brother and back to him, tears welling in them. "Is it Jhaia? Did something happen to Jhaia?"

Bo shook his head. "Your sister is fine. It's not her. You see, there was a spell to bind an ice god, no one knew what she intended . . . she saw that it was the only way . . . and by the time we realized it, there was nothing to be done."

Her gaze flashed anger at her brother. "Who? Tell me."

"Neima," Gheil said, his voice strangled. "She sacrificed her essence to save us all. She has joined the ancestors. She said she was at peace."

Layne rushed to hug her brother and then moved to him. The scent of her pain infuriated his beast, but there was nothing to be done.

"I'll plan her service," Layne said, wiping her cheeks. "Tell Jhaia she can help if she wishes."

CHAPTER NINETEEN

*C*olt rose from the depths, unsure of his surroundings and how it was possible that his consciousness remained whole. Well, whole wasn't exactly accurate—he was him, plus more. Avestaexa's powers still coursed through his veins, yet the presence of the god had diminished.

"That's it, cop. Wake up. Show us that yer still in there." The deep brogue of his Celt drew him from the cold darkness of his prison.

He swallowed, scanning the room and the expectant faces standing around the bed. It would be a total dick move to pretend he was still Avestaexa, and the daemon side of him was tempted. A much bigger part of him didn't want to waste the chance to speak to Brennus.

"Hey, B. What's new?"

Brennus chuffed and lifted both of their left hands. "Well, we got hitched, so there's that."

"And we kicked the ass of your ice god," Zander said, looking pretty damned pleased with himself.

"And you're pretty fucking naked," Seth added, tossing over a towel.

Colt flopped the towel over his lap and sat up. "Can we back up? What did I miss?"

Brennus filled him in on Ringo's drawing and Phoenix, Storme, and the Djinn seer creating the binding ring, and how Avestaexa had gladly accepted the ring as a token of the Celt's affection and devotion.

He held up his hand, wriggling his fingers. "So, this will hold him at bay?"

Phoenix shook his head. "No. If all works as planned, it ends his existence. Over the course of the next few months, maybe years, his ability to take human form will diminish."

"So, I'm free?"

"As long as ye leave the ring on yer finger, aye."

He stared at the general's ring, and his heart hammered in his chest. "I'll never fucking take it off."

"Then our work here is done," Zander said, holding his fist up for a bump. "Glad to have you back, my friend."

"Glad to be back," Colt said, giving up a round of fist bumps. "Thanks, guys. I'll never be able to repay you."

Zander snorted. "Did anyone record that? Once we get back into the swing of things and need you to clean up our messes, you'll be taking that back."

Colt waved his words away and shook his head. "Not a chance. I'm still gonna charge you for my services."

"There's the demon we know and tolerate," Seth said, heading for the door. "Laters."

And just like that, he was alone in his bedroom, looking up at a very tired and sexy redhead.

"Are ye really all right, cop?"

Colt flopped back onto the mattress and rolled onto his side, making room. When Brennus stretched out beside him, he brought the duvet up and cocooned them. "I feel like a few chapters of my life passed without me. I'm grateful, don't get me wrong, but how did they know the ring would work? How did they get the ring to you? How did you get it on his finger? The cop in me has my mind spinning, searching for answers."

Brennus set a warm hand on his cheek and yawned. "Neima, the Djinn female, knew the spell. Ringo drew the ring, so they knew that was the delivery method. When the buzzer rang, and I found Ringo in a Skip the Dishes outfit, holding a bag of food, I figured out PDQ what they wanted me to do."

"So, you proposed to me?"

"Down on one knee and everything."

Colt laughed. "Bullshit. You did not."

Brennus held up his hand, his fingers spread. "Scout's honor. I popped the question, and here we are."

Colt laughed harder. "That's the Vulcan peace sign, and you're not a boy scout. You can't shit a shitter, General."

Brennus yawned again. "Believe what ye will, I pledged my devotion and affection, and yer frosty side ate it up. It seems he'd believe anything if he's getting his ass kissed."

Colt sobered, letting the silence of his apartment sink in. He was free of his curse and got the guy. How did that happen? "When you say you kissed his ass . . ."

"Figure of speech, ye pervert."

Brennus's general braid slipped through his fingers as he stroked the Celt's hair. "Man, you said you'd get me through this, and you did."

"It was a team effort all the way round."

"I have some massive thank yous to deliver."

Brennus clasped their hands together and shifted closer. Facing each other, inches apart, he felt the warmth of the cop's skin. "We both do. Fer now, the only thing that matters is that yer safe and yer free to make choices fer the future. Life is good, cop."

As Brennus closed his eyes, Colt stared at their clasped hands and their twin rings. Yeah, life was better than he deserved, but he wouldn't complain. He'd never complain again.

~

It was four long, glorious nights before Brennus and Colt came up for air. They'd fucked, talked, made love, and made plans. With Avestaexa still a presence within Colt, they decided not to move into the ranch. Maybe in a year or two, when they knew for certain the danger had passed, and the family was safe, maybe then . . . or maybe they'd live the life of randy newlyweds for as long as they could.

"You sure there's no getting out of this?" Colt asked for the hundredth time. "I'm not on duty for another two hours, and I *really* want to try out those mattress straps."

Brennus escorted his mate into the foyer of the ranch, and bent to engage the retinal scanner. "Poor Martin. After signing off on yer online purchases today, I dinnae think he can take much more."

Colt laughed and followed him into the foyer. "Oh, he can take it. When we're alone sometime, remind me to tell you about the time I found him in the electrical room with his wife and the woman at the end of the hall."

"The blonde with the huge—"

Zander coughed and cut him off.

He turned to meet the gazes of the whole family, waiting in the living room to greet them. "Heart," Brennus said, finishing the sentence. "The sweet lady with the huge heart."

Colt busted up, and they went into the lion's den to face the well-wishers.

"Nice feathers," Seth said, pointing at his wings. "Hurt's like a motherfucker, yeah? So, how'd you get them?"

Brennus felt the heat of his blush color his cheeks, and cleared his throat. Other than his powers, the ice god left Colt one other modification. The pleasure barb at the base of his sac protruded from his cock during orgasm. When it locked hold, both of them lost their minds—cue one Dark Angel transition.

"File that one under none of yer business, Egyptian."

"TMI?"

Colt bit his bottom lip and looked around at the women in the crowd. "Oh, hells yeah. That's in the vault for life."

"Good enough for us," Zander said, pointing to the bar on the far wall. "Let's drink."

Brennus accepted the save and followed his commander's lead. "Yer speaking my language, Sumerian."

The next twenty minutes went on like that—hugging the wives, throwing back the shots, catching the hot glances his mate cast his way.

"And then," Colt said, his smile cocky, "he actually did drop to his knee and ask for my heart."

The resounding female *awwws* had him abandoning the shot glass and claiming the bottle.

"The best part was—and this proves our Celt is a hopeless romantic—he . . ." Colt's embarrassing recount ended as the charge in the air announced an unplanned visitor . . . well, three.

Brennus and his brothers all hit their knees as Lady Divinity appeared with her brother and a stunning blonde ghost—

"Mama?" Ronnie rushed across the floor and stopped dead in front of the group as Danel caught her arm. He stepped in between his wife and the Yin and Yang of the Otherworld.

"Forgive her," he said, bowing his head and pulling Ronnie to his side. "My mate is unfamiliar with the protocols of the Choir and overwhelmed to see her mother."

"There is nothing to forgive," Lady Divinity said. "I expect, seeing your dead mother for the first time in over a decade might be a shock to any one of us."

"Hi, Ronnie's Mama," Sunshine said, bouncing her head from side-to-side. "Did you come to sees my room?"

Danel bent down and scooped his orphan into his arms.

"You and you has the same hair," she said, pointing to the Dark Prince and his sister, Lady Divinity. "Are yous angels too?

Oops, I's not supposed to say that. Do you want to see my room? I gots a bed and a kitty. A real kitty. His name's Rascal. He scratched my arm."

Danel pressed a hand over the chatterbox's mouth and looked like he might melt on the spot.

Lady Divinity, however, seem to take no offense. "In a moment, child. First, I wish to speak to your mommy here."

Sunshine's face scrunched up. "My mommy's with the angels. Ronnie's my . . . what is you, Ronnie?"

"She's your mama," the blonde ghost said, winking at her. "And that makes Danel . . . ?"

"Kitty," she said, grinning from ear to ear. "He likes it when I calls him that. Kitty's a good name."

Lady Divinity laughed, and the sound of it put a smile on every face in the house. "While Kitty is a wonderful name, young one, perhaps your warrior might like to be your daddy."

Sunshine pressed her palms against his cheeks and squished his face. "You wants to be my daddy?"

The Persian swallowed. "It would be my greatest honor."

The kid looked around at the room, wide-eyed. "Does that mean he wansta?"

"Yes, monkey," Danel said. "I wansta."

Zane cried in the playpen, and the girl wriggled to get down. "My turn. Daddy, it's my turn to put the baby's sousie in."

Danel set her on her feet, and she ran off for baby duty.

"Apologies," Danel said, wiping a rough hand over his face. He gestured to the ghost and wrapped an arm around Ronnie's shoulder. "What's this about? Not that I'm complaining, but why is Scarlett here?"

Shayton shrugged. "I came for the booze and to check out this ring that bound Avestaexa. That fucker's been a thorn in my side since the beginning."

"And also, to wish the two of them well on their mating," Lady Divinity scolded.

"Yeah, yeah, that too." The Dark Prince peeled off, and he and Colt headed his way. "Although, all this love and family might make me hurl chunks."

Zander laughed. "You're not getting the good stuff if you're not planning on keeping it down, Shayton."

"Fuck you, Sumerian. Bring it."

As things devolved from there, Brennus poured another round and looked at the general chaos of his family. It seemed impossible that only two years ago, none of this was a reality.

No wives. No children. No Ringo. No home for them.

"Is it always like this?" Colt asked, shaking his head.

Brennus nodded. "Aye, it is."

And thank fuck for that.

~ THE END ~

If you enjoyed Brennus and Colt's story, please leave a quick review.

If you'd like to go straight into the final book of the series and witness Taharqa's love story, click here.

ALSO BY JL MADORE

Printed in Great Britain
by Amazon